For Dusty Lakeshore
and Squeaky Madison,
pornstars

SHANE SIMMONS
SEX TAPE

ISBN: 978-0-9952776-3-2

Sex Tape

Published by Eyestrain Productions
eyestrainproductions.com

EYESTRAIN
PRODUCTIONS

Prologue

January 1st

IT WAS COLD and cloudless, with a bitter chill to clear away the smog that would have normally reflected all the lights of the urban sprawl back down on itself. The sky was as black as it ever got over the city, and you could see the stars—plenty of them—but no one was stargazing. The yellow and orange sparks drifting around high overhead were brighter and putting on a better show. The first of the news copters was circling the scene, getting aerial shots that would debut on morning news shows from coast to coast. Everybody likes a spectacular four-alarm fire burning out of control over breakfast. Look what awful shit happened while we were sleeping, honey—glad we weren't there. They'll eat it up with their eggs and bacon. Some judicious editing might be in order to make the coverage family-friendly.

Mixed in with all the burning embers were glossy pages filled with pictures. Tens of thousands of magazines were helping fuel the flames as the block-long warehouse went up like a blazing pile of dry leaves. Tits and ass and beaver shots filled the sky for a whole mile straight up, riding the wind in the column of intense heat rising off the disaster area.

It was a porno inferno.

More sirens blared as emergency vehicles of all types kept arriving on the scene just in time to confirm there was nothing much they could do. The whole industrial park was a sea of flashing red lights, and the cops and paramedics huddled together in tight groups, watching the firefighters dump another million gallons of water onto a write-off they only wanted to keep from spreading. After a while they got tired of standing around with their thumbs up their asses, witnessing a fortune of smut go up in smoke, so a few of them decided to make themselves useful and went on a coffee run to the nearest donut shop.

And there was me, sitting on the back stoop of one of the ambulances, sucking air through an oxygen mask, fighting off smoke inhalation. Someone tried to get me to lie down on a gurney and I told him to fuck off between coughing fits. I didn't complain when someone else threw a blanket over my shoulders while I sat with my air tank and my take-out coffee, black. They said it was for the shock, I took it for the cold. Ten years in this icebox town, I still don't have a proper winter coat.

The thing about surviving a trauma like a car accident or an earthquake or a tornado is that everybody keeps asking you if you're all right. As if you're qualified to answer a question like that after a near-death experience. You're in such a daze, you're not even one-hundred-percent sure you survived at all. As far as you know, you're lying dead somewhere, hallucinating your own miraculous survival as the last few synapses in your brain burn themselves out.

Other than that, sure, I'm just fine. Thanks.

The next thing they want to know is if they can get you anything. Anything at all.

Yeah, you can actually. I know exactly what I want.

Dumbo

December 24th

CHRISTMAS IN MALIBU looks about the same as any other day in Malibu. The sand and surf are as far from seasonal as you can get, and the few attempts at holiday cheer—a plastic reindeer stuck in a lawn, some coloured lights hanging from terra-cotta shingles—seem hopelessly out of place. Even the carols ring hollow. It all feels like set dressing waiting for a film crew to arrive and roll out the sheets of artificial snow and throw around bags of synthetic flakes to complete the effect. If you close your eyes and let your mind drift, you can almost smell the sweat on the actors as they hunch over the air conditioning in their trailers. Then they pull on hats and scarves and go outside in eighty-degree heat to put on the performance of their lives—acting like they're cold.

Alexandra Middleton kicked open the door of the pool house with the tip of a designer shoe. Her arms were full of identically wrapped presents, each with a grand red ribbon to seal in their contents until morning. She could barely see her way past the stack until Jeffrey, ever the eager worker bee, ran over to unload her burden.

"For me?" he teased.

"One! Just one," Alexandra insisted.

"Which one?"

"Take your pick, they're all the same."

"Well, it's the thoughtlessness that counts," Jeffrey replied, as he delivered the new arrivals to the base of a giant silver Christmas tree over-adorned with so much bling it could be spotted from orbit.

The bee hive was buzzing extra loud in those closing hours before the holiday break. The inside of the pool house, which more often than not served as office space for the key staff of the Queen Bee, was only slightly less luxurious than the adjoining mansion. Unless guests were over and actively doing laps in the pool outside, the only changing that went on in the pool house was the constant swapping of portable hard drives and cell-phone batteries as staffers kept the hype flowing and the busy schedule of public appearances, interviews, screen performances, and recording sessions from tripping over each other.

Cindy was busy signing her way through a stack of eight-by-ten glossies of the glamorous movie star who didn't look anything like her. The lack of resemblance didn't matter, so long as the signature was a reasonable match to the genuine article. Patrick sat on the couch next to her, pairing photos with form letters and stuffing them into mailer envelopes. The photos wouldn't make it to fans in time for Christmas as originally hoped, but they would make for a happier New Year soon enough. If things weren't such a last-minute rush, Cindy would have made the extra effort to personalize each one. But it was Christmas Eve and she had a plane ticket booked, so there was a limit to how magnanimous she was willing to make her employer appear.

"Slow down," said Patrick, "you're scribbling."

Cindy dropped the pen and shook out her hand.

"Writer's cramp," she announced. "Let me get a shot of muscle relaxant."

The pool house came equipped with a well-stocked bar and a large punch bowl full of heavily spiked eggnog had been prepared by some thoughtful soul who believed the holidays were best celebrated in a stupor. Cindy got up and scooped herself another cup.

Jeffrey's phone rang with a copyright-infringing tone.

"Yeah? No. I don't know. Hold on," was as far as his conversation got before he tried to pass it off on Monica. Monica was already switching back and forth between two separate phone calls on two separate phones.

"Right. I'll just grow a third arm," Monica bitched and turned her back on Jeffrey, refusing the third call.

"God, I need a drink," said Alexandra, who had already had her fill of the chaos in thirty seconds flat.

Cindy came over with a couple of brimming cups and offered one.

"Eggnog?"

Alexandra sneered, "Is that a trick question?"

"Scrooge."

"Scrooge needs something with some kick," said Alexandra, eying the bar, scoping out whatever hadn't been siphoned away in the name of holiday cheer and the need to survive it all with some sanity left intact. "Scrooge wants tequila."

Patrick held up one of Alexandra's identical gifts to his ear and gave it a good shake. He heard nothing that offered a clue.

"Can I open this now before I get too drunk to remember who it's from?" he asked.

"So much for playing secret Santa," said Alexandra, too busy wringing the last few drops of tequila out of a bottle neck to intervene.

Following Patrick's lead, the others started digging into Alexandra's presents, tearing through a store clerk's meticulous assembly-line wrapping job. They all found copies of the same book resting inside tissue-laden boxes. The title declared:

Take It from the Top: The Helen St. Simone Story

The photo on the cover was nearly identical to the one Cindy was signing—slightly younger, a little more airbrushed, and in colour—but otherwise the same face, the same smile, the same monument to everlasting youth, vitality, and Botox.

"Oh, that's so generous!" Monica gushed, "Just what I never wanted."

"No wonder secret Santa wanted to maintain her anonymity," added Patrick.

"I think I would have preferred a lump of coal," Cindy concluded.

Jeffrey sniffed at his copy of the book.

"Fresh from the printer," he said, "I love that new-paper smell."

Monica flipped open her book and fanned through the pages, inhaling deeply.

"Really?" she said, "All I smell is bullshit."

"Hey hey, come on," Alexandra tried to defend herself against the onslaught. "I worked long and hard to get these masterfully told lies on the shelves in time for Christmas."

"Thank you, Alex," said Patrick, doing his best to muster some token gratitude, "I'm sure it will make a lovely doorstop."

"Where is Helen the Hun anyway?" said Alexandra, looking around and noticing a degree of ease and levity usually missing from the grounds.

Cindy flipped through the year's itinerary, filled with notes and amendments on coffee-stained and dog-eared pages. There were only a few more relevant pages to go before the notebook could be retired and the new one, already half-full of dates and schedules, would suffer the full brunt of daily abuse.

"Prague still," said Cindy after a few moments of deciphering her rushed scrawl that filled the page for December 24. "I think. You know, the thriller that wants to be The Da Vinci Code on half of the budget."

"And none of the brains," Monica added. She was all too familiar with the project and had held it in disdain when it was still being shopped as a bad first draft. Ten worse drafts followed before the Queen Bee committed.

"Too close for comfort at any rate," said Jeffrey, who couldn't find Prague on a map and was only slightly reassured by that fact.

"Let's hope they forgot to put film in the can and need to do all sorts of re-shoots," said Alexandra.

"Hear, hear!" Monica raised her cup of eggnog to this notion and took a sip. She spat it back out a moment later and went into a coughing fit. The rest of the staff gathered around her, concerned, slapping Monica on the back, offering her healthier beverages, and generally making sure her airway was clear. Monica couldn't speak, so she pointed with her eyes. One by one, the others followed her gaze to the window. Somebody was outside.

A moment later, Helen St. Simone blew onto the scene, her phone in one hand, a thousand-dollar bag with accessory dog in the other. She was in the middle of a heated conversation with someone she referred to, with no amount of ironic affection, as "cunt-face." It could have been anybody.

She was on the wrong side of forty, working hard to maintain the body of a twenty-year-old. Exercise and diet covered most of the bases, but makeup and surgery had been picking up the slack as the years rolled by. Slowly but surely time was winning, and if you looked closely enough, the seams were starting to show. No one got close enough to look anymore. Helen was a phenomenon best appreciated from a safe distance.

Killing her call with a sharp stab of her thumbnail, Helen stopped in her tracks. She tipped her sunglasses forward on her nose so she could have an unobstructed view of all the holiday trimmings.

"Fuck me," she declared. "It's Christmas already?"

"Welcome back, Helen," said Patrick, a pained smile etched onto his face as pleasantly as he could manage, "How was Prague?"

Helen tossed her phone into her bag. Accessory Dog ducked out of the way of the missile fired by his mistress.

"Foreign. Very fucking foreign. Why in the fuck they need to shoot movies in these butt-fuck nowhere banana republics is fucking beyond me!"

"Architecture? History?" Monica forwarded.

"You want history? Build it on a fucking sound stage!"

Jeffrey and Patrick chuckled hollowly at what they assumed was Helen's attempt at humour.

"Okay, cut the crap. What do we have lined up?"

Cindy hurried to consult her agenda, flustered when she felt Helen's icy attention shift to her.

"Not much," said Cindy, after a few short moments of hurried scanning. The pages were all in her own handwriting—some of it meticulously neat, some of it a frantic chicken scratch. The chicken-scratch notes came from particularly busy days and ranged from vitally important engagements to forgotten lunch orders jotted down when there was no other paper handy.

"It's the holidays," explained Cindy, when she could feel the impatience building in the room. All of it was Helen's, but it was pushing the air out. Cindy flipped one more page back and forth, double checking both sides like she was determined to find some essential appointment in a coffee ring. "I didn't know for sure when you'd be back so I've been keeping things open."

"I'm back now," sneered Helen. "This is me, back. So put your ass in motion and let's get busy! Is my caterer booked yet? Flowers, music, cake?"

Cindy's voice downshifted from uncertain to meek, "Nobody's around to take my calls. Everyone's out of town by mid-December."

Alexandra saw Helen boiling over into her wrath-of-God mode and tried to deflect it with her own update—a petty ego stroke that might distract the Queen like a fistful of ground beef might distract a large angry wolf.

"I got you a magazine-cover shoot for the day after New Year's."

Helen's willingness to be distracted was conditional.

"Which magazine?"

"People," said Alexandra. It wasn't a lie, but she said it like a kid in math class who had just picked a random number to answer a teacher's unexpected question.

"Again? When the fuck are you going to get me an Oprah cover?"

"I'm pretty sure only Oprah gets to do O covers," said Alexandra, soft peddling some harsh reality for someone who never took reality well.

"Tell that egomaniacal cunt to move her fat ass over and let someone else have the cover for once! It's not like the whole fucking magazine isn't already named after the bitch."

Explosion over, Helen instructed Alexandra more civilly, "Make the call, she'll do it for me. We're tight."

All the while Alexandra was running interference, Cindy had been rifling through her agenda, hunting for something that might satisfy Helen. She had met with very limited success.

"The closest thing I have scheduled is the dress. That's the second week of January."

Alexandra was surprised to hear Cindy speak again. After jumping on a grenade for her, she didn't expect the dumb kid to pull another pin so soon.

Even Accessory Dog sensed the coming storm and ducked down into his bag for cover.

"The dress? Now? Are you fucking kidding me? Do I look like I'm at my wedding weight yet? I'm not ready to be fitted for a fucking dress!"

"Well, I...I could..." Cindy began, but she came up empty. She was too rattled to recover. The rest of the staff took a collective step back, keeping out of the line of fire.

"This is a spring wedding! Get your shit together because I'm not getting married in the middle of an L.A. summer! I want flowers in bloom and songbirds! Not brush fires and melted catering!"

"Okay, so I'll put a hold on the dress, I'll call catering and..." Cindy was already tripping over her own mental list. "Who else?"

"Fuckwit! I've been away for three weeks and what have you done? Fuck-all!"

Cindy tried to stammer a response, but all she could manage was the word, "Pen."

She looked around ineffectually. "I'll just grab a pen and..."

"I'll handle this myself!" insisted Helen, digging for her phone. Accessory Dog yelped in terror as his mistress's dagger-manicure clawed around his lair seeking its prey in the maze of beauty-enhancing and age-masking gadgets. She came up with it moments later and found who she wanted on speed dial.

Helen was connected to an answering service.

"We're sorry, our offices are closed for the holidays," explained a recorded voice that didn't sound the least bit sorry. "If you'd care to leave a message…"

Cindy had crossed the room in search of a pen. With one finally in hand, she was hurriedly amending her agenda with fresh chicken scratch.

"Fuck it!" announced Helen, who had already decided she didn't care for the recorded voice and outright hated whatever out-of-work actress was behind it. "Here! You talk to them!"

Helen launched her cell across the room with force, nailing Cindy squarely in the back of the head. Cindy was knocked off her feet by the surprise blow and fell to her knees, cupping the point of impact with her hand.

Helen pivoted on her heel and stormed out of the pool house with a parting, "Merry fucking Christmas!"

Only when the boss was safely out of earshot did Monica raise her cup of eggnog and respond, "Happy fucking New Year."

Cindy was still on her knees, her face turned away from her co-workers, crying softly to herself.

"Buzz kill," said Jeffrey, giving the whole ugly scene his personal epitaph.

Alexandra walked over to Cindy, not sure what to say. The girl wasn't hurt badly. Not physically. But she was a wreck just the same. It had been a long, trying year toiling under the St. Simone brand name. Alexandra picked up Helen's phone and turned it off.

Patrick was the first to try to dispel the unpleasant atmosphere that permeated the room. "I know what can clear the air. Lighten the mood. Give us all a holly-jolly Christmas..."

Jeffrey perked up immediately.

"Dumbo?" he asked, not even trying to contain his delight.

"Dumbo," agreed Patrick.

"Oh please, not again!" groaned Monica. Her eyes rolled so far into the back of her head, they appeared only white and bloodshot.

The boys could not be dissuaded. With no further prompting they began chanting, "Dum-bo, Dum-bo, Dum-bo!"

"It was entertaining the first fifty times, but seriously, it's wearing thin."

Monica's attempt to stem the boys' mounting enthusiasm failed to penetrate their increasingly loud and insistent mantra. Alexandra glanced back at Cindy. She was on her feet again, but still obviously upset.

"I'm sure we could all use a laugh right about now," she said. Patrick and Jeffrey stopped chanting and looked at their co-workers in frozen anticipation.

Monica threw up her hands, resigned. "Fine, I've been out-voted. Just let me pound down a few more drinks before you make me sit through this magnum opus. Again."

As Monica hit the bar for a refill, Alexandra opened a cabinet under the widescreen LCD that was mounted on the wall. Inside was a selection of Helen

St. Simone DVDs, some of them ten- and even twenty-year anniversary special editions. A smattering of the selection included a few that didn't benefit from any sort of St. Simone participation: well-watched personal favourites, freebies from gift bags, or unwatched Academy screeners for voting members. Digging past the top layer of the movie library, deep into a forgotten core of defunct formats, Alexandra arrived at a stack of disused videotapes. All of them sported colourful oversized packaging once common in the children's section of the video store. These were the sentimental selections Helen had bought for herself when she first arrived in Hollywood, back when she was still capable of sentiment. For a while, they had served to remind her of a simpler, happier time in her life, before money and fame made everything so complicated. Many years later, she still hadn't bothered to upgrade her collection of animated classics because she no longer cared to be reminded of her childhood. The only things she now associated with her early history were pimples, extra pounds, and obscurity. It had all been carefully glossed over in her new authorized biography—a pastiche of invented memories that foreshadowed great success several chapters hence—and that's how she liked it.

Alexandra selected one VHS case from the dozen in the back. "We'll watch some edited highlights. Then it's going back in the Disney vault for another year."

She opened the case. The tape inside did not match the packaging. It was an anonymous no-name brand VHS tape, unmarked except for a simple masking-tape label on the spine. Handwritten was the single word, "Dumbo."

Patrick rummaged through a closet for the old forgotten VCR that lay buried under boxes of financial records and inflated tax write-offs, saved in anticipation of an audit no one wished to live long enough to see. Various audio and video cables dangled out of the back of the unit from the last time it was hooked up, making for a quick and simple plug-and-play.

"Cindy, go round up the usual suspects," said Jeffrey. "You know who the fans are."

Cindy wiped away a few remaining tears as she went out the back door to seek a broader audience. She put on a brave face, but was failing to get caught up in the festive mood of this holiday tradition.

▶ ▶▌

It only took about fifteen minutes to gather the troops. Everyone was always game to join in the Christmas festivities. By the time the winter break came around, they had all endured another year's worth of Helen Hell, and were eager to once again bear witness to the campy, charming, vulgar disgrace that was "Dumbo."

Helen's inner circle had been joined by Pierre, the long-suffering chauffeur who could never get more than two blocks without wanting to weld the partition between himself and his backseat driver shut; Anna, the long-suffering maid who was expected to pick up all sorts of things after her boss, including enough grams to get her busted for felony possession; and Ramon, the long-suffering pool cleaner and gardener who had become the sexual harassment poster boy of the group despite publicly outing himself to his persistent boss with a string of buff boyfriends. Other irregular attendees included the fiscal-quarter accountant, the local paperboy, and the current body-guard in a string of sacked security personnel that had come full circle twice.

Drinks were served all around, and couches and chairs had been dragged in front of the television so everyone could enjoy a front-row seat. Patrick confiscated the string-of-popcorn garland off the Christmas tree so he could snack on one stale kernel at a time. Every time he popped another bone-dry piece in his mouth, he had to be careful not to choke to death for all the laughing.

The room was in an uproar of contagious hysteria. Everyone there knew the contents of The Tape by heart, word-for-word, grunt-for-grunt, groan-for-groan. Even if they hadn't been to every screening, they had memorized the contents through osmosis. Snide references and in-jokes worked their way into staff conversations throughout the year to the point that some could have recited the whole thing before they ever got to see it for the first time.

Like a screening of a cult classic, the fans knew to put a hold on their gales of laughter when one of their favourite bits was coming up.

"Say it! Say it, baby. Say it for Daddy," said the panting man on the tape. Some of the viewers silently mouthed the words along with the performers.

The woman on the tape responded hesitantly, shyly, "Fuck me. Fuck me, Josh."

The grunting and the panting resumed at a quickened pace, but no one could hear it above the howls.

Monica had arrived at that sweet spot where she was just drunk enough to appreciate the comedic value of the video she'd already seen too many times.

"I can't believe Helen had to be coaxed into dropping an f-bomb back then," she said.

It was a poor line reading, but Helen had gotten better since her early days in town. She had the Oscar to prove it. It was one of the special Academy Awards they give in the category of "Best good-enough performance by a lead actress who probably should have already been given an Oscar for a better movie but hasn't and now it's kind of embarrassing because she's so hugely famous. Oops." Nevertheless, it was a golden statuette, lobbied for by a major studio and agreed upon by industry peers who were too frightened of her to see her lose again.

"You think her tits were real here?" said Patrick, who was so over the shock value of The Tape that he had long-since moved on to a more technical analysis of the contents.

"No," said Alexandra, "but they've definitely had upgrades since."

"Seriously, how many times have we watched this now?" asked Monica.

"Well, every Christmas for what, eight years?" said Alexandra, the only one sober enough to count. "Plus a number of special occasions."

"Not to mention private screenings," added Jeffrey.

Jeffrey felt the room's eyes on him. No one remembered being invited to a private screening.

"You know, when no one else is around," Jeffrey tried to clarify. His eyes remained fixed to the screen as he hugged a cushion intensely.

"Jeffrey?" asked Patrick delicately. "How many times have you seen it?"

"All told? Thirty-seven. It just gets better and better."

The moment never had enough time to get awkward. Monica was pointing at the screen and hopping in her seat with excitement.

"Oh! This is my favourite part!" she squealed.

The room fell dead silent so they could hear every nuance of the next immortal moment in secret-cinema history.

"No, Josh," said the woman on the tape, "Please. Not there. It's dirty."

The audience exploded in laughter again, a cathartic release of energy, an exorcism of built-up anger and frustration. Better than sex. Certainly better than the inept, fumbling sex performed for a video camera so many years and so many crimes against humanity ago. The Tape only improved with age.

Cindy, sitting on the far edge of the couch, resting her head in her hand, was the only one not enjoying herself. Her face was still streaked with dried tears, and although she was watching the video along with everyone else, she did so through cold, detached eyes. Her thoughts were not with the groping couple on the screen from years before, nor with her co-workers in the here-and-now. She was thinking ahead, towards some future time in a faraway place, where the abuses of a self-absorbed tyrant would be a faint memory. It was an idle fantasy, toyed with many times. Only now did a plan to arrive there start to form. It was sketched out in considerable detail twelve-and-a-half minutes later when the tape came to an abrupt end with a jumble of video noise and snow. The auto tracking on the VCR struggled to adjust to the next image on the tape—the end of a late-night infomercial for a product everyone wanted back then that had since become a forgotten artifact of the last century.

The entire staff burst into a round of sarcastic applause and Jeffrey looked for the remote control to stop the machine.

Through her mock tears, Monica declared, "I love a happy ending."

Within moments, everyone had their phones and hand-held devices out to check the time or call loved ones. It was getting dark out quickly.

"Okay, everybody, it's officially Christmas Eve," Patrick announced. "Go home to your families. And if you don't have a family, I hope Helen's stellar performance has inspired you to get busy with somebody special tonight and start one."

Monica downed the final drops of her last drink, toasting, "Here's to more of the same shit in a whole new year!"

Patrick made an addendum to his holiday wishes, shouting it across the room for maximum embarrassment. "Jeffrey, your right hand does not quality as 'somebody special.'"

A one-finger salute was the only acknowledgement he received in return.

Alexandra hit the eject button on the VCR and returned the tape to its case, filing it away in its place of forgotten honour in the TV cabinet. When she rose again and turned, she found Cindy watching her closely. Her eyes darted away the moment Alexandra looked back at her. At least the waterworks appeared to be done with for the evening.

Alexandra was in no rush to get home to her husband and kids. There were none waiting. Just a plump Persian cat named Sabrina, and she had plenty of food and water in her bowls to hold her over. After spending the better part of an hour tidying up the pool house, Alexandra stood out on the patio, looking at the city lights twinkling in the distance. It hardly felt like the holidays, but she was sure it would sink in after a week of not doing much of anything. By New Year's morning, she might even feel relaxed enough to dread going back to work for a whole new round of stress and chaos. The thing she most feared about time off was getting used to it. Liking it. The thought made her shudder in the warm breeze.

Cindy was the only other staff member still straggling. She set the alarm system in the pool house and shut the door behind her. It locked automatically. Swinging her bag over her shoulder, Cindy tried to slink away quietly to her leased compact parked in Helen's enormous oval driveway. Alexandra wouldn't let her get away without a parting, reassuring word.

"Take it easy, Cindy. I'll see you in the New Year."

Cindy stopped and briefly debated with herself about how much she should say.

"No. You won't," she stated matter-of-factly. "I'm going back home to see my folks over the holidays. And then I was thinking about finding an apartment somewhere in their neighbourhood."

"Oh come on, kiddo," Alexandra tried to laugh it off. "You're not going to let that little bit of ugliness with the bitch-goddess of the universe chase you out of town, are you?"

"No, I'm going to let the five-thousand identical scenes over the past nine years do it."

"Has it really been nine years already?"

Alexandra wondered if she was more shocked that she'd known Cindy for almost a decade, or that she was nearly a decade older than when she first met the promising but naïve waif and felt compelled to take her under her wing. She'd thought, at the time, that she was far too young to be playing the role of mentor. Now she felt too tired to ever imagine herself taking on that sort of responsibility.

"It's my own fault," Cindy sighed. "I was the one who wanted to get into show business. Instead I got stuck in the rut of being a celebrity minion. I think it was glamorous for the first couple of years. After that, famous or not, a shitty boss is a shitty boss."

"I could ask around." Alexandra was stretching. "I have other clients. They might be looking for someone."

Cindy knew who Alexandra's other clients were. None of them were half as famous as Helen St. Simone, nor half as well staffed. And nobody in town wanted a personal assistant who had already been broken in and then broken down by a bigger name in the business. Cindy was damaged goods and she knew it.

"I think I'll pass," Cindy said, but they both knew it was Cindy who had been passed over.

"You going to be okay?" Alexandra's question held none of the fake concern for another person's well-being that so often fuelled professional relationships in the industry. She still had a soft spot for the girl she'd once thought she could offer a leg up to.

"Sure," said Cindy with a smile that was faint but genuine enough. "Just as soon as I put some time and distance between me and this place."

"Take care," Cindy added, as she walked away down the patio, led only by the light of the underwater pool floods. Through the pathway gate and fading into the darkness of the vast property, she was gone in moments.

Flight

December 25th

ALEXANDRA SLEPT WITH only two things of consequence. The first was her night mask, which sheltered her eyes from the harsh L.A. sun that blasted through the closed blind slats over her bedroom's east-facing window every morning. The second was Sabrina, who curled up at her feet each night on the same spot that was always marked with the plush white fur that had been shed since the last laundry day. On special occasions she would sleep with a third thing—a pill or two to keep her down for the count when she really needed her rest. The weeks leading up to the holiday break had been exhausting enough that chemical assistance was unnecessary to make the eight-hour quota of beauty sleep. These days, Alexandra would have preferred a solid ten hours each night to preserve her looks and her sanity. Maybe now, with a whole week free…

It wasn't the sun or Sabrina's yowling hunger pangs that woke Alexandra first thing on her first morning off. It was the phone, of course. It was always the ~~goddamn phone~~. She ~~reached for it without even~~ bothering to lift her mask to check the time. Her internal clock was already telling her it was too early for this shit. Especially on Christmas.

"Alex, I'm sorry to call today of all days, but there's been a robbery at the house."

The voice on the other end was Jeffrey, and he sounded genuinely apologetic enough for Alexandra to not want to tear him a new one. A small one, perhaps.

"Helen's house?" she asked, although she already knew it couldn't be anyone else's. The police would normally have gotten the call first, but if it involved Helen, there was probably going to be damage control to manage before any cops were summoned. That was covered under Alexandra's broad job description as her publicist.

"What's missing?" was the next question. As long as the answer wasn't something irreplaceable like an Oscar, a Grammy, or Helen herself, there was nothing that couldn't be rebought without making much of a dent in the balance sheet.

"Some jewelry, some cash," said Jeffrey.

Manageable, simple. Alexandra made no effort to rise. "Was it a break-in?"

"No. They had a key and the code. I called everybody as soon as I found out."

Jeffrey tapered off. "Alex?"

"Yeah?"

"I can't reach Cindy. She's the only one."

"She quit last night," Alexandra told him. He was the first she'd mentioned it to. She figured it was bad news that could wait until everyone else had enjoyed a worry-free break.

"So what do we do?" asked Jeffrey. "Call it severance pay and hope Helen never notices?"

Alexandra sat bolt upright. The violent motion frightened her cat, who ran to hide under the dresser.

"Oh, my God," she said to no one in particular and tore off her night mask. The room was very bright, despite the closed blinds, but Alexandra didn't even squint in the sudden light.

"What?" Jeffrey sounded troubled. He knew Alexandra was unflappable at the best of times. This sounded like the worst of times.

"Has anyone checked on Dumbo?"

▶▶❘

Alexandra got out of her car and walked up the drive to the grounds of Helen's mansion. She felt like she had just left. The rest of the key staff—Monica, Patrick and Jeffrey—had beaten her there. They were gathered outside by the pool.

"Really, it's okay," said Monica, who couldn't contain her sarcastic impatience. "My kids can finish opening their Christmas presents tomorrow."

"Stow it, Monica," snapped Alexandra. "Your kids will have a happier holiday if mommy still has a job to come back to."

Everyone gave Alexandra her space as she looked down at the flat stones that made up the patio area around the pool. Silently, she started counting them from one particular stone that was a little darker than the rest. Six stones in, seven over, Alexandra bent over and started to pry up the edges of one that looked identical to all the rest around it.

"Wait, what?" Patrick was confused. "Nobody should be getting fired over this! It's not our fault!"

"Don't worry. Nobody's getting canned. Nobody's getting blamed."

"Thank Christ for that," declared Jeffrey, reassured by Alexandra's words.

Under the stone, pressed into the earth beneath, Alexandra retrieved a Ziploc bag with a key inside. She let the stone fall back into place.

"Our jobs are probably going to disappear all on their own if we don't put a lid on this," Alexandra clarified.

The others flocked around her as she plucked the key out of the bag and unlocked the pool-house door. A jumble of questions spilled out of the trio, challenging Alexandra's logic with a fear that escalated the more they worried she might be right.

Alexandra threw open the door and looked inside. Nothing appeared to be disturbed, but that meant little. The alarm system beeped to the beat of everyone's pounding heart. Patrick typed the code into the keypad, disarming it.

"Meet me in the situation room," said Alexandra, striding straight to the television cabinet.

"We have a situation room?" It was news to Patrick.

"Today the kitchen is the situation room," Alexandra told him.

"We're probably pushing the panic button for nothing," said Jeffrey, who always took it upon himself to find a way to be unrealistically upbeat. "We don't even know it's missing."

Alexandra tore through the stacks of DVDs and videos until she found the Dumbo case exactly where she left it. She opened it and looked inside.

The empty VHS case was tossed onto the granite island in the middle of Helen St. Simone's sprawling kitchen for all to see. The hollow plastic shell rattled across the surface until it came to rest next to one of the three redundant sinks. The staff all stared at it with a dread that was growing with each passing second. Amidst their feeling of sinking horror, they all turned to Alexandra for leadership. Or least a feeble attempt at reassurance.

"You're the publicist," said Patrick. "Tell us, is this good publicity or bad publicity?"

"I thought there was no such thing as bad publicity," said Jeffrey, remembering an old quote he had once thought sounded profound.

"Ask O.J. if he agrees with that," grumbled Monica.

"Maybe it's not such a bad thing," Patrick speculated. "I mean, other than letting the whole world know Paris Hilton is a lousy lay, it didn't do her career any harm. Such as it is."

Monica liked where this was going. "No one thought any more or less of Pam Anderson. All I remember anyone talking about was the size of Tommy Lee's dick."

"R. Kelly got burned, but only because he was banging jailbait," offered Jeffrey.

Alexandra said nothing. She was making calculations in her head.

Finally she asked, "What are we pushing in the new year?"

"Soda pop and cosmetics," said Monica, who had worked hard to land those contracts. The Helen St. Simone brand was an easy one to sell, but Helen herself less so. Especially when clients came forewarned about how she could be a tad "difficult."

"The pop is definitely going to dump the contract if it gets out," concluded Alexandra. "How slutty is the makeup?"

"What do you mean?"

"Is it whore makeup or classy makeup? What demographic is the cosmetics company targeting? Skanks or ladies?"

Monica wasn't sure. She looked to Patrick who was better at keeping track of the finer details while she closed the deal.

"Skanks?" he asked himself, trying to remember the campaign pitch. "Yeah, skanks."

Alexandra sighed, relieved. "Okay, good."

"Teenage skanks," Patrick specified.

"Fuck!" declared Alexandra. "They're still going to want a wholesome spokesmodel to appeal to the wholesome moms of the teenaged skanks. What movies do we have lined up?"

This was Jeffrey's department. "Just some voice-over work," he reported.

"Good. No biggie." Alexandra sounded genuinely relieved.

"For a feature cartoon," added Jeffrey.

"Fuck! What's the TV show we've got going?"

"The CSI de jour?" Patrick knew the one. "It's called 'Lockjaw.' Helen plays a deaf forensic dentist who can't remember her past."

"Tell me it's for subscriber cable." Alexandra was grasping at straws now.

"Network and affiliates."

"Fuck!" was Alexandra's final verdict.

"Okay," she said, sitting down heavily on one of the kitchen stools, "there's no way this tape can come out now. Every development deal and promotion we've got going will take a shit."

"How long is this going to put us on the outs?" asked Monica, who was thinking about how far away she was from paying for her children's college education many years down the road.

"You've seen the tape," said Alexandra. "It's not a pretty picture. We can come back from that, but it's going to take time. I've been selling Helen as America's sweetheart for too long. Rebuilding a whole new image on the ruins of a sex scandal... You can't do that overnight."

"How are Helen's finances?" Jeffrey said, expecting more bad news.

"What can I say? The bitch likes to spend," was Monica's answer. "There's not much in the coffers right now. If we lose contracts, there'll have to be cutbacks. Maybe you, maybe me, maybe all of us before this thing blows over."

"How long are were talking?" asked Patrick.

"The whole town is going to take a step back from Helen St. Simone," said Alexandra. "We're talking at least a year or two. And that fairy princess wet-dream wedding at the end of May? Count on that gravy train being casualty number one."

"That would be tragic," said Monica, ever the sentimentalist. "You know what they say. You only get married for the fourth time once."

A depressed silence fell over the room. It was during this quiet moment that Helen came wandering into the kitchen in her bathrobe. She was groggy, with her hair all over the place and her face still waiting upstairs in a series of emollient jars. Without acknowledging anyone, she opened the fridge and retrieved half a grapefruit resting in a bowl with a serrated spoon. Only after she had her breakfast in hand did she notice that she wasn't alone. The revelation did not faze her—Helen so rarely had a moment when she wasn't surrounded by her wranglers that she only really took notice when nobody was there at all.

"What the hell is everybody hanging around for?" was all she wanted to know. "I thought today was a holiday."

"We just came in to sort out a couple of work issues," Alexandra told Helen. "Nothing you need to concern yourself with."

"Good. Well, fuck the grapefruit," said Helen, tossing the bowl and spoon into the nearest available sink with a horrid clatter. "Since you're all here, somebody can make me pancakes. I'll be in the gym burning them off."

Helen wandered off again in search of some exercise equipment that could preemptively balance a decadent calorie-and-carb invasion of her body-temple. As soon as her back was to the staff, they all flipped her the bird in choreographed unison before turning their attention back to the pressing business at hand.

"I figure the only shot we've got at stopping this shitstorm is to track down Cindy before she does something stupid with that tape," said Alexandra.

"Do we call the cops, or what?" asked Monica.

Patrick was horrified by the suggestion. "Are you kidding?" he said. "You might as well send out a press release while you're at it. We have to do this in-house."

"Do we have any idea where she's gone?" asked Jeffrey.

The staff exchanged a lot of blank stares. They only knew Cindy from work. Few personal details had surfaced, despite all the hours they had logged together. In the industry, everyone liked to talk about where they were going and what they would do when they got there. Few people liked to talk about where they were from, or where they were stuck at the moment. That sort of information wasn't for work friends. It was reserved for people who could be considered real friends.

Alexandra was the only person in Los Angeles who Cindy thought of as a real friend.

Back at her condo, Alexandra spooned the contents of a can of cat food into a dish that was custom printed with the name "Sabrina." Once that task was done, she shook a single tiny pill out of a bottle of prescription medicine and pushed it into the middle of the goopy wet tuna-flavoured mess. She finished burying it with her fingers and then set the bowl down on the floor. Sabrina immediately trotted over and greedily began gulping down her lunch.

Alexandra returned her attention to packing. She already had a couple of overnight bags halfway stuffed with changes of clothes, and another big case locked and ready to go. Jeffrey was there to offer assistance and condolences.

"Sucks you having to fly on Christmas," he said.

"Jewish. Don't care," answered Alexandra.

Scoring last-minute tickets on one of the busiest travel days of the year had cost her a fortune. It had been a lucrative year of commissions doing the publicist hustle, and Alexandra consoled herself that she could use a big fat expense to deduct. She just hoped she'd never have to explain the exact nature of this impromptu business trip to a nosy taxman.

Jeffrey watched Alexandra pace back and forth between her closet and her luggage, piling in more and more wardrobe options. She seemed to be preparing herself for any eventuality between a safari and an inaugural ball.

"So…Montreal. You ever been?" Alexandra sounded more nervous than Jeffrey had ever heard her. This was stepping into a complete unknown. It was even worse than the time she had let Helen drag her to a PETA singles mixer held at a gay bar in Portland. Montreal was a best guess, but Alexandra was pretty sure Cindy once claimed it was her home turf and that her parents still lived there.

"No. You?"

"Never been to Canada, period," said Alexandra. "I like beaches and sun when I go on vacation."

"You go on vacation?" Jeffrey's surprise sounded sincere, but Alexandra ignored the comment just the same.

"Montreal's in Canada, right?" Alexandra took a brief moment off from packing to second guess her limited geographic expertise. The entire east coast of the continent blended together into a vague grey zone in her mind.

Switching to the bathroom, she started gathering her toiletries for the trip.

"Who do we know there?"

"Nobody," said Jeffrey, but then a second thought occurred to him. "Well…"

"Who?"

Jeffrey thought better of opening old wounds. "Forget it."

"Give me a name. Anybody. I don't even speak the language."

Alexandra took another moment off to second guess her limited understanding of east-coast culture, which blended together into another vague zone so grey it bordered on black.

"They speak French in Montreal, right?" Alexandra didn't particularly care if it was a stupid question. She doubted Jeffrey knew for sure either.

"There's Sid," said Jeffrey, ignoring the less-pressing query.

The mention of Sid's name stopped Alexandra cold in the middle of her packing flurry.

"Oh, God," she said, "I forgot all about Sid. So that's the rock he crawled under, is it?"

"It was about as far as he could run without crossing an ocean."

"Still not far enough for me," Alexandra sneered with distaste. She stuffed a can of hairspray into a vacant corner of her bag with a certain unnecessary violence.

"You want his number?"

"Hell no," Alexandra practically spat her words. "If I ever want to find Sid Volke again, I'll just look for the trail of slime. Anyone else?"

"Not really. Not so many runaway productions run away there these days. It's gone out of fashion."

"I guess I'll just have to recruit my own native guide when I land."

Alexandra checked on her cat's progress. Sabrina sat next to her bowl. It had been licked clean except for the pill resting untouched at the bottom.

"How does she do that?" wondered Alexandra aloud. "Help me hold her still."

She lifted Sabrina onto her kitchenette counter. Jeffrey held the cat as Alexandra squeezed the pill between Sabrina's clenched molars and forced it down her throat.

"Num num!" she coaxed. "Here comes the choo-choo train."

"What's that for?" Jeffrey wanted to know.

"Kitty Valium. It helps relax her on the plane."

"You know you could get a pet sitter for a couple of days. I could look in on the little monster," Jeffrey offered, quite magnanimously he thought.

"I never leave my baby with anybody. Ever."

Sabrina was still trying to scramble away after her forced medication, but Alexandra held her fuzzy face in her hands and made kissy faces at the cat.

"Isn't that right, sweetie?" she asked in a voice that came nauseatingly close to infantilized.

"Is that a trust issue or a biological-clock issue?" asked Jeffrey.

Alexandra let Sabrina dash off and hide. She'd be easier to cram into her portable cage in a few minutes once the pill started to work its magic. "I can't leave her alone on Christmas."

"I thought you said you were Jewish."

"I am," said Alexandra. "She's not."

With effort, Alexandra managed to squeeze another bag shut and latch it.

"You know, I envy you," said Jeffrey.

"What part? Me having to clean up this mess during the holidays, or me being a heathen on the biggest birthday-party bash of the Christian calendar?"

"You heading up north. How great is that? You get to spend the holidays in a winter wonderland."

It was pouring rain. Alexandra stood at the Arrivals platform of Trudeau International and tried to hail a cab. Apparently few cabs cared to be out in such poor weather.

As airports went, Montreal's was quite spacious and modern and not at all like the arctic landing strip she had expected. She understood, dimly, that it had been recently renamed after a politician or political cartoonist or somebody who made a good caricature. Even so, everyone was still calling it "Dorval" after the suburb it was situated in.

Alexandra had passed through customs and retrieved her bags in less than an hour. Sabrina was curled up in the back of her cage. The effects of the pill were wearing off, but she was still stoned enough to not particularly care how cold and wet it was out. It looked like the middle of the night, but it was only early evening, and had already been dark for hours. This was December above the 49th parallel. At long last a stray cab came by, cruising for straggling fares. The driver popped the trunk, but made no effort to get out and help Alexandra load her bags. When she was finally done, she hopped in the back with Sabrina's cage and shook the rain out of her hair.

"I got off in Canada, right?" Alexandra asked the driver. "Where's all the snow?"

She hadn't seen a flake since her plane dipped below the cloud cover and ran straight into sheets of water. The only snow in evidence was on a poster in the airport that advertised the glistening white slopes of a ski hill a couple of hours' drive out of town.

The driver spoke in a heavy Eastern European accent and told her, "Snow come and go last week. Is rain now. Maybe tomorrow is ice."

"Any recommendations for a place to spend the night?"

"You want come home with me?" asked the driver with a slight smile.

Alexandra could see him glancing at her in the rear-view mirror to make sure she took his comment as a joke. He was also checking just in case she found it charming. She didn't.

"I was thinking more along the lines of a hotel. Alone—thanks just the same."

"You make reservation?"

"No. This trip was a last-minute thing."

"You want good or want close?"

"Too much to ask for both?"

"Driving in this shit, close better than good."

Alexandra looked out the window. Visibility was poor and more dirty water splashed across the cab's windshield with each pair of hazy headlights that streaked by.

"Close wins," declared Alexandra, and took out her phone to dial a few digits.

▶▶❙

Alexandra was still punching in numbers, navigating directory assistance, when they arrived at the motel. It was a two-level design dating back to the mid-60s, conveniently close to the airport and inconveniently close to the sound of landing jet planes. When Alexandra finally made the connection she was looking for, she had to speak loudly to be heard over the air traffic above.

"Mrs. Gauthier?" Alexandra asked, butchering the French Canadian name to the point it sounded more like "goat ire."

"Hi, my name is Alexandra Middleton. I'm a friend of Cindy's from L.A. Your daughter, Cynthia? That's right."

Alexandra had dreaded trying to hurdle the language barrier, but was to relieved to discover she could understand Cindy's mother just fine. The accent was thick, but more comprehensible than an average Celine Dion interview.

"I was in the neighbourhood so I thought I'd look her up," explained Alexandra. "I know she came home for the holidays."

She paid the cab and left most of her bags just inside the door of the lobby, out of the rain. The only thing she brought with her to the front desk was the cat carrier so Sabrina wouldn't have to suffer the weather. Setting the cage down on the floor, she made eye contact with the manager, prompting a polite but indifferent response.

"Room?" asked the manager. He wasn't much in-volved in holding up his end of the transaction either. An ancient compact radio hung heavily in his breast pocket, and an earpiece was letting him keep up-to-the-minute with the World Juniors hockey score.

Alexandra flashed the manager a thumbs up so she wouldn't have to break away from her phone conversation. She was hearing a lot of confusion from the other end and a quick-fire exchange in French between Cindy's mother and father.

"No? Really?" It was Alexandra's turn to join in the confusion. "I was sure she said something about going home for the holidays. Well when was the last time you spoke to her?"

"Single or double?" asked the manager.

Alexandra held up two fingers and tossed her gold card onto the desk. The manager turned the registration book around for her and swiped the card through a reader.

"Thank you, Ms. Meyerhardt," he said as he returned Alexandra's card. She winced at the mention of her non-professional name.

Alexandra grabbed a pen to sign in but stopped before she could set it down on the next blank spot. One name a few lines up from the bottom had drawn her attention.

"Well well well," she said, quite pleased with herself.

"Madame?" the manager said.

"Thank you, Mrs. Gauthier. I'm sure I just got the dates wrong," said Alexandra, disentangling herself from the unproductive call as quickly as she could. She hung up.

"The girl in room twelve…" Alexandra asked the manager, "Late twenties, skinny with short black hair?"

"You recognize the name?"

"No," said Alexandra. "The handwriting."

Cindy hadn't checked in under her own name, but Alexandra had seen that same scrawl on a thousand Helen St. Simone headshots and a thousand pages of scheduling notes. She'd know it anywhere. Even here, at the ends of the earth.

▶▶❙

The motel was badly understaffed, and at this time of night, the manager was all there was. Claiming he had to watch the front desk, he offered no assistance moving Alexandra's luggage until she tipped him generously in U.S. dollars. After that he became quite chatty and helpful, hurrying to carry everything to her first-floor double, two bags at a time, and providing her with unsolicited updates on the hockey game. Alexandra left him to it, not wanting to be around when he got to her heaviest bag. That was the one with her emergency travel supply of cat litter. It had been close to eight hours of commutes, airports and airplanes to get here, and by now, anesthetic buzz fading, Sabrina must have been dying to pee. The cat would have to wait a little while longer to relieve herself. Business came first.

While the manager transferred her bags and readied her room, Alexandra took Sabrina and went around the side of the motel to find the stairs. The rain was starting to let up as she climbed to the second-level walkway and found the room number she was looking for. She knocked lightly.

"Cindy?" she said, "It's Alex. Open…"

Just knocking on the door was enough to make it swing in.

"…up."

Alexandra stepped into the room. The air inside was hazy and she fanned her hand in front of her face, coughing.

"Damn girl, what are you smoking in here?"

Alexandra thought Cindy had quit. She'd arrived in L.A. as a nineteen-year-old habitual chain smoker who had already been puffing away for years. Barring the occasional lapse, years of patches and nicotine gum had gotten the tobacco monkey off her back, but she'd still take a drag if someone passed her a joint at a party.

Taking a second breath, Alexandra realized it was neither cigarettes nor pot she was smelling. Something was burning.

Alexandra put the cat carrier down and shrugged her purse off her shoulder. Only one lamp was on in the room, but there was enough light to see the waft of smoke coming out of the bathroom. She found the source in the sink. A wad of crumpled-up paper was resting next to the drain, a few licks of flame trying to consume the final bits of fuel. Alexandra ran the tap, putting out the fire. She flipped a switch on the wall to turn on the vent fan and the air began to clear.

Alexandra stepped back outside the bathroom where it was a little less smoky. Only then did she see the pair of feet sticking out from the space between the twin beds. She leaned forward so she could get a better look and saw Cindy lying there with a length of cord pulled tight around her neck. Her face was frozen in contorted agony, and there were self-inflicted scratches on her neck where she had tried to dig her fingers under the garrote to pull some slack. Fresh blood glistened on the scratches and Cindy's face was bright red, even though she was clearly dead. There had been no time for the fluids to settle, or for the body to grow cold and pale.

This just happened, was the only thought Alexandra could form before she was struck from behind. She was so transfixed by the sight of her friend lying dead on the motel carpet, she hadn't noticed the sound of shower-curtain rings sliding across their bar in the bathroom. Someone had been hiding in the tub, curtain drawn, waiting for the intruder who had walked in on a crime scene in progress to turn her back for a moment.

With Alexandra distracted, the man in the tub seized his chance to make a break for it. He elbowed her out of his way, hitting her in the side of the head, hard. She landed on the floor across from Cindy's body, and the impact knocked the wind out of her. There was a grunt of pain from the assailant as he grasped his bruised elbow, but it didn't slow his escape. Lying on her back, dazed, Alexandra looked up behind her in time to get a fleeting upside-down glimpse of the man tripping over the cat carrier on his way out. Sabrina couldn't decide whether to yowl or hiss, and her alarm at this violent jostling came out as a mix of both.

Alexandra tried to scramble to her feet, but it took several long seconds to get her bearings after such a sharp and unexpected blow to her skull. She stumbled outside and fell heavily against the second-level railing, just in time to see the man running away across the wet parking lot below, splashing through puddles at a full sprint. He was out of sight a few seconds later.

"That's pretty much all I saw," said Alexandra. "Just the colour version, from a slightly higher angle."

It had been two hours since the murder and the assault. Alexandra's head felt a little better, but Cindy was still very much dead. It had taken the first uniformed cops only ten minutes to arrive at the motel. Police detectives showed up soon after. There had been a lot of questions since then about what exactly had gone on between Alexandra and Cindy, and it seemed like she had won the prime-suspect sweep-stakes until the manager remembered the motel's security camera. After a tedious period of rewinding and fast-forwarding the outdated video surveillance system, they found the image and the time code that backed up Alexandra's story of a third person in the motel room. Black and white footage showed the figure of a man fleeing the scene. It was so close to Alexandra's mental image of the event, she figured the camera must have been fixed to the balcony she'd been standing on, almost directly underfoot.

"But you didn't see his face." It was a statement rather than a question from Inspector Langelier. He'd already asked half a dozen variations of the question, and Ms. Middleton nee Meyerhardt had only offered an extremely unhelpful middle-height, middle-build description.

"I got a good look at his elbow," was her response, the most sarcastic of her descriptions to date.

Ice from the ice maker spilled down into a waiting towel with a crisp rattle. The motel manager wrapped up the towel and knotted it, handing it to Alexandra to replace the previous ice pack that had since become too soggy. She nodded a thanks and held it to her head where she'd been hit.

"Is this the only camera angle you have?" Langelier asked the manager.

"The only camera, period," the manager told him. "Front parking lot, twenty-four/seven."

Alexandra looked out the window and saw a pair of paramedics trying to get their gurney and its sheet-covered occupant down the wet stairs without slipping. It looked like a couple of broken legs waiting to happen. They froze, in precarious place, to let a coroner squeeze by, lugging his medical examiner's bag. Once the delicate maneuver was accomplished, he came into the front office to report to Langelier.

"Anything interesting?" the Inspector wanted to know.

"Minor contusion on the back of her head."

"Was it the cause of death?"

"No, it's recent but not new. Everything else is consistent with strangulation."

Langelier let the coroner leave and he returned his attention to Alexandra.

"How long did you know the victim?" he said, continuing his line of questioning.

"Coming up on ten years. I got her her first gig in L.A."

"And what brings you to Montreal?"

"I came to find Cindy. She left abruptly, on bad terms."

"She was fired?

"She quit."

"How much was she paid in severance?"

"Nothing. Why?"

The Inspector reached into his coat pocket and removed a plastic evidence bag he'd been handed half an hour earlier by one of his men who had just completed a preliminary sweep of the room. It contained the corner of a soaked slip of paper. The edges were burned away. He showed it to Alexandra.

"What is it?" she asked.

"Looks like a cheque," concluded Langelier.

Alexandra took a closer look and recognized what little was left of the sheet she had doused in the sink. There was a figure in a printed sum box. The hand-writing was non-descript. Given the size of the number, it certainly wasn't something Cindy could have written herself.

"Looks like a lot of zeroes," Alexandra commented.

"You didn't write it?"

Alexandra scoffed. "Remind me to show you my bank balance some time."

"I will. Next time we talk. You're staying in town?"

"I wouldn't want to miss this lovely weather you're having."

Langelier considered whether he had any more pressing questions to ask before locking up the crime scene and moving his people out. There was one.

"What's the final?" he asked the manager, who still had the radio plug stuck in his ear.

"Seven-three, us," was the quick response.

Langelier showed little reaction but nodded knowingly. Alexandra figured they were speaking in code. It had been a long day and an even longer night and she felt no desire to try to crack it.

The manager placed a comforting hand on Alexandra's shoulder and asked, "Can I get you anything else?"

Alexandra curtly cut through the kindness.

"The number of a good hotel. Five stars, no dead bodies."

Boxing Day

December 26th

ALEXANDRA HAD STAYED in a good number of five-star hotels over the course of her hobnobbing career. It was still too early to judge how this one stacked up, but it was certainly a three- or four-star upgrade from where she'd begun her northern excursion. After such a violent and horrific arrival, she'd decided she surely must be suffering some degree of post-traumatic stress syndrome, and therefore needed to pamper herself accordingly. The honeymoon suite was available, so she splurged and then promptly ordered every frill and extra the stately old hotel in the heart of downtown Montreal had to offer. Alexandra was digging her personal credit hole down to the clay, but she figured she'd earned it. Deserved it, dammit.

A lengthy nap born out of pure exhaustion had turned into the sleep of the dead, without a single dream, troubling or otherwise, to disturb it. A long bubbly soak in the suite's spacious Jacuzzi had melted away most of the aches and pains air travel always generated. Alexandra continued to suffer a dull throb where she'd been elbowed in the head, so she decided the only cure for that would be an in-room spa treatment.

While Sabrina snoozed, curled up on a stack of pillows on the king-sized bed, Alexandra reclined on a settee wearing only a plush hotel bathrobe, a towel to wrap up her hair, and a pair of cucumber slices over her eyes. Two aging Asian women worked on her finger- and toenails using a vast selection of emery boards, each with a specific grain designed to sand away the roughness on anything from a robin's egg to tree bark.

With her free hand that had already been manicured to perfection, Alexandra lazily reached for the phone to call down to the front desk. She fumbled for the receiver in her cucumber-induced blindness, but soon made the connection.

"Hi, I'd like to order some room service for the honeymoon suite," she told the concierge. "Something with lots of chocolate."

Alexandra had no interest in interrupting her private spa to consult the menu that was sitting all the way across the suite. It didn't matter. The concierge was perfectly happy to rattle off a number of suggestions and a personal recommendation for the woman who was currently the top-paying client in the entire hotel.

"Yeah, that sounds good," she said, responding to one dessert that used the word "chocolate" three times in its deliciously descriptive title, "I'll have one of those."

"No, make it two," she corrected a split moment later. "I'm on the mend and need my strength."

Alexandra hung up the phone and tried to get back to some serious relaxing, but found she was already on the outside of her happy place, looking in longingly. The trance of euphoric bliss was broken as the first worry about work and the mission at hand wormed its way into her mind. Good food, a good sleep, and the talents of two wizened Chinese ladies with magic fingers and no conversation weren't enough to keep away that nagging sense of professional responsibility. This moment was wonderful, but barring that, Alexandra knew she was off to a disastrous start. Cindy was dead, Dumbo was missing, and she herself was battered and bruised and, if not for a timely piece of evidence to the contrary, would currently be enjoying the inside of a zero-star holding cell as a murder suspect.

She needed to find a guide, fast. Someone who knew their way around town and could not only speak to the locals, but to her as well. So far she'd met very few people, none of them promising. Other than a manicurist and pedicurist who only spoke Mandarin, a Slavic cab driver who barely spoke English, and the manager of a dive motel who only spoke hockey, there was no one on her radar. If only there had been more time, she could have done the research to come up with a viable alternative to what she was now forced to consider. But there was none. No time to do the legwork. Not even enough time to get her nails filed to a velvet finish.

Alexandra fumbled for the phone once more.

"It's me again," she told the front desk. "Right. The triple-chocolate-mousse-explosion-whatever lady."

She couldn't even hope to repeat the name of her order back at the concierge, it was so complex. "Can I get a side order with that?"

Alexandra shored herself up for the request. A necessary evil.

"The Yellow Pages," she said.

The neighbourhood is turning to shit, thought Claude, as he sat in his parked car, smoking like it was a race to beat his personal best. There was a time, and not very long ago, when the whole area was considered too residential to attract beggars. There were shops and grocery stores and innumerable small restaurants, but it wasn't a major hub of economic activity beyond the people who lived a few blocks above or below the main drag.

The area was an established part of the megacity, but was still two entire districts away from what was generally thought of as the City of Montreal. The main commercial zone was centred around a strip of Saint Catherine Street where the maze of underground shops let out onto a busy surface full of more shops and theatres and defunct department stores that had been divided into many new specialty stores. There, the best corners had been staked out ages ago. Some of the key panhandlers had owned the prime spots for years, with no intention of abdicating except in the case of death or serious illness. The busiest metro entrances were sewn up tight as well, and begging inside the subway system was strictly regulated by the Société de transport. Only the better buskers, with some real talent and decent instruments, were allowed to book a time and space in the common areas away from the platforms where the trains passed. Anyone who just wanted to hold a hat for a handout was denied.

The result was that the upcoming generation of economic victims and drifters was pushed farther and farther away from the urban core. Sherbrooke Street cut through centre-ville and continued west, all the way through Westmount, Notre-Dame-de-Grâce, and Montreal West, so panhandlers had started colonizing this obvious route, spacing themselves out at regular intervals to try their luck in these uncharted miles of loose change and abandoned deposit bottles and cans. Enough were making a successful go of it that they had become permanent fixtures.

Claude had come to recognize some of the vagrants by their distinctive layers of discarded winter clothing. But there were always new ones arriving on the scene, claiming a free spot, and waiting to see if anyone who owned a nearby storefront would try to shoo them away. It had become a game for Claude to spot the ones who would end up working the area regularly, or pick out the ones who didn't stand a chance and would soon migrate west, towards a warmer city. They were the washouts. The ones who had fucked up their lives so bad, they weren't even good at being homeless.

Like that one, Claude thought, as he focused on one particularly scruffy lowlife standing outside the automatic doors of a chain supermarket. The scumbag was a mess of greasy hair and week's growth of stubble that walked the fine line between unshaven and a full-blown beard. A shaggy moustache suggested he'd been growing that longer and more intentionally, but it was only a few days away from getting lost in the rest of the unkempt forest. His ratty coat looked very thrift shop, and would have been chilly in the fall, months earlier. In wintertime, even as wet as this winter had been so far, it was hopelessly out of season. Especially if you were planning on standing outside all day holding a Styrofoam cup and eyeballing strangers.

A good Samaritan, or perhaps just a pensioner with an active sense of social guilt, came out of the supermarket with her bag of groceries. She still held her change in her hand. When she saw the bottom feeder hanging around the exit, she counted the coins and thumbed off the lower denominations into his cup—nickels and dimes. Whatever social conscience nagged her, it didn't extend to quarters, loonies or toonies.

The bum didn't offer her any thanks, didn't even nod an acknowledgement. The Samaritan went on her way with no reward for her contribution to the underprivileged, tiny as it may have been.

What an asshole, thought Claude. Then he saw the beggar take a sip from his cup and realized he wasn't a beggar at all. He was the man he'd come to meet, waiting patiently with his cup of takeout coffee. Given the nature of his business, Claude should have guessed this is exactly what he would look like. It was repulsive, but entirely appropriate.

Claude got out of his car, threw his cigarette butt into the gutter, and approached the man.

"Are you Mr. Volke?" he asked, already quite sure, but figuring it was best to seek confirmation just in case it turned out there was no need to engage the filthy degenerate in further conversation.

"Yeah, that's me," Sid told him, and took another hit of his pocket-changed flavoured coffee.

"I spoke with your secretary on the phone a few times about a job I might have coming up."

Calling her a secretary was pushing it. Sid paid a weekly stipend to a woman who worked a phone-sex line from home for extra cash. She was a nearly unilingual-French single mom-of-three named Marie-Louise Somethingorother—Sid had long forgotten. Marie-Louise was a fiftyish shut-in with a unibrow and a couple hundred extra pounds she dragged

around her cramped duplex on twin canes. On the
phone she sounded half her age, a quarter of her
weight, and about a million times as hot. Despite her
very limited English, she still took Anglophone calls.
Marie-Louise only had about a two-hundred word
English vocabulary, but she knew all the dirty ones
and how to deliver them. Sid gave out her number
as his own, piggybacking his business calls on her
dedicated line. He only got a few calls a week at best,
so it rarely interfered with Marie-Louise's paying
customers. Whenever she got a call that wasn't a
breathless man trying to give her his credit card
number, she wrote down what they said and left a
lost-in-translation message on Sid's answering service.
The details were usually wrong, but as long as she got
the phone numbers and addresses right, it all worked
out more often than not.

"She mentioned," said Sid, who had only gotten
her first message about the job that morning. "Extra-
marital, right?"

Claude nodded.

"Marie-Louise told you my rates?"

"Yes," said Claude, who had gone comparison
shopping looking for inexpensive and had settled on
outright cheap.

"When were you thinking about getting started?"

"Right now," Claude told him. "She's in there.
With him."

Claude's hands were stuffed in his jacket pockets for warmth, so he pointed at the apartment building across the street with his chin. A stabbing motion.

"You brought a camera?" he asked Sid.

Sid pulled a battle-hardened digital camera out of his inside coat pocket and flashed it to Claude just as another sort of lowlife might have flashed a gun. It was neither the latest nor the greatest model, but it still got the job done in a high-enough resolution to hold up in any court of law.

"Always," he said.

Sid looked across the street at the apartment building. It was a bland, brick low-rise, four storeys tall, typical of veteran housing of the late 1940s. Now it was low-income housing waiting to attract the attention of condo developers so it could be reborn as unaffordable housing.

"So they're in there right now?" Sid asked. He struggled to find a way to put his next question delicately. "Together…?"

"Fucking, yes," agreed Claude indelicately. "I need quality photos. As high a DPI as that thing will go, with a clear view of their faces. Can you manage?"

"Which apartment?" was all Sid needed to know.

"Go down that side alley. It's the third window, first floor."

Sid always found this sort of thing so much easier if there was a convenient window to peep through. It was too easy, actually, and Sid grew suspicious.

"If you were here already, why call me? You could have snapped a few shots yourself."

Claude hung his head in shame, staring at the icy pavement. "I…can't," he stammered. "You see…well. This is sort of embarrassing, but, you know…"

It was painful to watch so Sid cut him short. He knew how humiliating it was to have a spouse cheat on you. Seeing still pictures of the action was hard enough for most husbands. Watching it live and in person was unbearable.

Sid gave Claude a reassuring pat on the back and told him, "I understand. Don't worry, I've got it covered."

He trotted off across the street, now officially on duty.

"I'll meet you after it's done," Claude called after him.

Sid made his way down an alley that was formed by one side of the building and a tall wooden fence that marked the edge of the next lot. It was lined with a series of trash cans waiting for pickup. The first floor was raised so that the basement dwellings would only be half a flight of stairs down. As a result, the windows were too high for Sid to peer through, even on his toes. He could tell the blinds of the third window were up, but could see no more than that.

Sid threw back the last of his coffee in one gulp and then dumped the hot, wet coins at the bottom into his hand. He pocketed the change and tossed the cup. As quietly as he could, using the broken slats of the neighbouring fence as a foothold, he stepped up onto one of the trash cans. The aluminum lid buckled and groaned but held. Carefully, he distributed his weight by placing his second foot on the lid of another trash can. Both cans were stuffed full of enough garbage bags that the thin metal lids didn't fold in on him. It was a delicate balancing act, but once he was sure it would hold, the two cans made a suitable platform that brought Sid up to eye level with the window.

The action between Claude's wandering wife and her young lover was just about exactly what Sid had expected to see, right down to the sexual position. There was just something with cheaters and doggie-style that simply went together, like peanut butter and jelly, politics and corruption, or sex and money. Today it would be their sex and his money. A match made in heaven. Sid made sure the auto flash was off—something that had burned him more than once—and started snapping digital photos of the event. He got the face shots, he got the body shots, he got the whole damn thing, hot and heavy. He'd been a silent observer of this sort of tryst so many times before, it no longer sparked anything more in him than purely clinical interest. Nevertheless, he took his work seriously and was so engrossed in capturing it all for posterity—and whatever future legal teams might become involved—that he didn't realize he was no longer alone in the alley.

Suddenly, the frantic fornicating in the apartment was interrupted. The bedroom door flung open and Claude burst into the room. Apparently he'd been unable to contain himself. The lovers froze in the act as he pointed a finger at them and started yelling accusations that were muffled through the closed box-windows.

"I knew it!" was about as much as Sid could understand from the man who had become his employer only five minutes earlier. Sid had noticed Claude practically vibrating with nervous anticipation over this sting operation, but he had read it wrong. He figured Claude had it together and would patiently wait in the car for his photographic evidence to be delivered. But with nothing to keep his mind off what was going on only a stone's throw away, other than holiday repeats of afternoon radio talk shows, Claude must have lost his shit. The jealous husband was lunging forward to physically accost the pair of cheaters when Sid was jolted out of the moment by a familiar voice.

"Sid Volke," it said, stating the obvious.

Sid tumbled off his garbage-can perch and landed on his ass in the slush and filth of the alleyway. He found himself looking up at Alexandra, who seemed far too pleased with herself for having caught him in the act.

"Still peeking through people's windows, I see. Is it business or pleasure?"

Sid rose to his feet, brushing himself off. It was a futile effort. The old dirt had the new dirt hopelessly outnumbered.

"Both," he said. "It's a pleasure when I get paid for taking care of business."

The altercation happening just above their heads got loud. There were raised voices all around and several heavy thumps. Alexandra gestured up at the scene they couldn't quite see.

"Anybody famous?"

"I don't do celebrity jobs," Sid told her. "Not anymore."

"Why not?" asked Alexandra, genuinely intrigued. This was not the Sid Volke she remembered. Back when he worked the Hollywood scene, he was the most tenacious paparazzo in the business. Everything was a celebrity job. There was no other kind of job.

"Anybody who wants to be famous is inherently unstable," said Sid, sharing the lump sum of wisdom he'd gained over too many years of chasing movie stars and rock idols from club to club, hoping one of them would do something shameful so he could pay his rent. Almost on cue, they always did.

"Everybody today wants to be famous," replied Alexandra, sharing her own accumulated wisdom from the publicity game.

"That's why the whole world is nuts."

The tussle above got louder and more intense. Personal possessions could be heard getting knocked down and broken.

"This sound unstable," observed Alexandra.

"At least it's real."

"And I'm not?" Alexandra sounded like she just might have had her feelings wounded a tiny bit.

"You're real enough," Sid told her. "But you work for celebrity phonies. Which one sent you?"

"I came looking myself. You weren't easy to find."

"You could have looked me up in the Yellow Pages and asked my secretary where I was."

"I did," said Alexandra. "But her English is atrocious."

Alexandra smiled smugly at Sid, but he gave her nothing.

"So," she continued, "You want to let me hire you for old time's sake?"

"Who are you working for these days?" Sid persisted.

Alexandra evaded the direct question. "I have a stable of clients."

"You have a bunch of nobodies who'll dump you the moment they get big. Who's your meat and potatoes?"

Alexandra couldn't tell if Sid was guessing or if he'd made a point of keeping well informed, even out here in his self-imposed exile. She decided it was best to come clean, just in case he already knew the answer to his own question. A bit of transparent truth went a long way towards building bridges in her line of work. It was a rare and precious thing.

"Helen St. Simone."

"I'm not interested," replied Sid immediately. There wasn't even a moment of consideration.

"You sure?" Alexandra made certain there was no hint of desperation in her voice. She tried pushing some of Sid's buttons instead. "It's a job with your name all over it. Very cheap and tawdry, you'll love it."

"Not interested," said Sid firmly, pronouncing each word as its own unshakable statement of fact.

There was still a lot of thumping and grunts coming from the struggle above. It had become loud enough to make conversation difficult, so Alexandra agreed to let it lie there. Aside from not wanting to try to talk over a group assault, she thought it was generally the best strategic move available to her.

"Your loss," she said. "I'll let you get back to your domestic misdemeanor."

Sid began to mount his trash cans again as Alexandra turned and walked back down the alley towards the street. He couldn't resist a parting shot of sarcasm.

"What, no business card? No phone number in case I change my mind?"

Alexandra didn't bother to turn or slow her pace. "You're the professional snoop," she called back at him, "It's your turn to find me."

And she was gone. Sid tried to get his mind back in the game and readied his camera as he looked through the window to see what he'd missed.

The lovers were back to banging doggie-style, but now Claude had joined in. He was naked and hammering away at the tail end of the threesome. They were all moaning and groaning and doing serious damage to the bed.

"What in the name of fuck…?" Sid asked himself.

He didn't know what surprised him more—the unexpected three-way or that something like that was still capable of taking him by surprise. It was difficult to swallow for a man who wore his cynicism like a hard-earned badge of honour.

Having your wife cheat on you is humiliating, sure. Watching it live and in person is unbearable for most husbands, but thrilling for a select few. Sid had seen it before but hadn't pegged Claude for the type. Especially the type who arranged it as foreplay and then jumped right into the fray knowing a stranger would be taking pictures. Sid's job made him feel like a whore and he was at peace with that. He often played the part of impartial observer and documentarian, but he'd never been dragged into a sex act as an unwilling participant before. Now he felt more like a raped whore, and he was not at peace with that at all.

Sid sat on the hood of Claude's car, fuming quietly to himself. Claude, his wife, and the young lover all came out of the building together twenty minutes later. They were freshly showered and had probably done that together as well. Now they were chatting like old pals, much more intimately than one sexual encounter would allow. Sid wondered how many other snoops and spies and private dicks they'd suckered into playing boudoir photographer for them before he got the call.

Claude broke off from the group and approached Sid, looking very pleased with how his afternoon went.

"Did you get it all? Close-ups, action shots?" he asked eagerly.

Sid remained silent. He took out his camera, popped open the hatch at the bottom, and ejected the memory card. Hopping off the car, he handed it to Claude and walked away without saying a word.

"You'll invoice me, right? Personal cheque okay?"

Sid never looked back.

Strip Search

December 27th

NIGHT HAD FALLEN, the clock was ticking. Alexandra didn't know how long she had to retrieve Helen's stolen goods, but the time felt short. The tape was out there somewhere. She had neglected to mention to the police that she searched Cindy's room and bag with no luck before they were even summoned. She hadn't told them about the existence of the tape at all. If it ended up confiscated as evidence, that was a sure way to guarantee it got viewed by everyone in the precinct, copied for additional personal review, and inevitably leaked to the public.

Someone knew where it was. They probably knew exactly what was on it. And soon, so would the whole world. There was nothing to do but try to get some sleep in her pricey honeymoon suite and wait for the seed she'd planted to sprout.

Alexandra was in a deep coma with Sabrina curled up at her feet. The sudden loud ring of the hotel phone next to her head dragged her back to the waking world, but the cat never moved a whisker. It took five rings before Alexandra could muster a concerted effort to reach for the receiver.

"Mmm?" was all she could manage as an answer.

It was the night watch at the front desk.

"I'm sorry to disturb you this late, Madam, but there's a call for you. He says it's urgent."

"...okay," Alexandra grunted.

There was a click as the call was patched through. Alexandra didn't wait for the other end of the line to speak first.

"Sid, what took you so long?"

Sid hated being so predictable, but he knew he'd have to eat some attitude from Alexandra once he finally forced himself to make the call. He played it cool.

"Mostly the soul searching. Finding you was much easier. I would have called on your unlisted cell, but I figured it would be more polite to go through the front desk."

Alexandra tipped up one eye of her sleep mask to check the time.

"At three-thirty in the morning. Very thoughtful."

She figured it was equal odds that Sid was lying about tracking down her unlisted number. Either way, it showed he still had the goods. Snooping or bullshitting, he could do either proficiently, and he'd probably have to do lots of both to get this job done.

"Let's talk about your offer over breakfast," said Sid.

"Only fishermen and paperboys have breakfast at three-thirty in the morning. How's eleven sound?"

"Six," Sid lowballed.

"Eight. Final offer," said Alexandra with an employer-to-employee firmness.

"I'll be waiting downstairs," Sid told her and hung up.

Alexandra did a poor job of returning the phone to its cradle and then buried her head back in her pillow for another few hours' sleep.

Sid held the business card in both hands and inspected it carefully. It was a far-east bit of etiquette he'd picked up from a Vietnamese investment banker he'd once done a divorce case for. It was meant to show proper respect for the person who had made the humble offering of their title and contact information printed out in convenient card form. Eastern etiquette or not, Sid was unable to hide a look of derision. He liked the tactile sensation of the soft fibres under his thumbs, and the embossed lettering was sharp enough to cut yourself on, but he'd already spotted one big fat lie, which brought all the other information it contained into question as far as he was concerned.

"Who the hell is Alexandra Middleton?" he asked, already knowing the answer. Already sickened by it.

Alexandra sat across from Sid at a table in the hotel's restaurant, sipping coffee and poking at the remaining crumbs of her morning muffin.

"That's me," she said.

"What happened to that bright-eyed Orange County go-getter, Alexis Meyerhardt?"

"Too Jewy, even for Hollywood," replied the long-since self-christened Alexandra Middleton. "Middleton is my stage name."

"You're not an actor," Sid informed her.

"Wanna bet?" Alexandra countered. "In my line of work I have to be a little bit of everything. Mother, father, psychiatrist, best friend. It's the only way to get some of these superstar basket cases to hustle their wares and make us some bucks."

"Best friend, huh?" Sid sounded unconvinced. "From what I hear, Helen St. Simone doesn't have any friends."

"That's where the acting comes in. Right now, though, I'm the best friend she has in the world. I'm such a good friend, I haven't even troubled her with where I am and what I'm doing here. The less she knows about it, the easier it will be for her to deny everything if it gets out. At least she'll sound more convincing while she's lying."

"So you're the real actor. She's just the movie star."

"Oh, she can act just fine if you give her twenty takes and a trailer full of perks," said Alexandra. "But when the press shows up for a scandal and parks their camera trucks on your lawn, they only give you one take. And they hope you blow your lines."

Sid tucked Alexandra's card down one pocket of his wallet and fished around inside for something that would reciprocate the formal exchange. He found what he was looking for in the bill fold that contained no bills, only assorted Canadian change that had worn the fabric to tatters.

"This is me," said Sid, slapping down a piece of paper on the table.

Alexandra picked it up carefully with the tips of her fingernails, careful in case she might infect herself.

Sid's own business card was flat only by virtue of having been pressed in his wallet for so long. Dog-eared and discoloured, it looked like it had been crumpled up and flung back at him more than once. It may also have been dropped in a bowl of soup at some point. Alexandra guessed minestrone.

The name "Sid Volke" and the ambiguous term "consultant" were the only bits of information printed on the card. There was also a phone number, but it had been scratched out a rewritten in ballpoint pen several times.

"You can keep that," Sid told her.

"Thanks. No," replied Alexandra, and dropped it back on the table.

Sid look relieved at not being separated from his longtime companion. He collected his business card and returned it to the darkest enclave of his wallet where it would wait patiently until summoned, and likely rejected, once again.

Sid was getting tired of the dance. "So are you going to tell me what this impending scandal is, or do you want me to guess?"

"I need to know you're onboard first," was all Alexandra would offer.

"Sure I am. Probably. If it's really juicy."

"With your signature on a non-disclosure agreement," Alexandra added.

Sid leaned back in his chair, pushing away from the table, repulsed by the suggestion. "Oh, come on, Alex. I haven't signed a legal document since my divorce. And you know how well that turned out."

"No name on the dotted line, no juicy details."

Alexandra finished her coffee and got up. She wasn't sure if she had Sid on the hook yet and there was only one way to find out for certain. She walked out of the restaurant without saying goodbye.

Sid sat at the vacated table, trying to decide if he really wanted to chase after her. Apparently he did. Sid found himself on his feet and hurrying out the door before he could make a count of ten. Alexandra was waiting at the elevators by the time Sid caught up with her.

"Look, this scandal you've got—whatever it is— it's nothing to me," promised Sid. "I've seen them all. I've even done a few myself. They all boil down to two things. It's either sex or drugs. Both on a good day."

"This one got an upgrade," said Alexandra as the elevator arrived. She stepped on board and pressed the button for her floor.

"To what?" Sid asked, unable to picture anything bigger or better offhand.

"Murder," answered Alexandra.

The elevator doors closed, leaving Sid behind.

▶ ▶❚

When the doors opened again, eight storeys later, Alexandra was only mildly surprised to see Sid still standing in front of her. He was breathing heavily and sweating hard from his sprint up the stairs.

Sid had just enough breath left to tell her, "Okay, you've got me intrigued. A bit. A little bit." He held his thumb and index finger slightly apart, emphasizing "bit."

"I have the non-disclosure papers in my room waiting for you," Alexandra told him. She never went anywhere without a boilerplate N.D.A. in with her business documents. You never knew who might hear or see the wrong thing and need shutting up.

Alexandra pulled out her passkey as she approached her suite. Before she could swipe it, she saw that the door was already ajar. The wood around the frame was splintered and the door itself was cracked where it had been kicked in.

Inside, the suite was destroyed. Bedding and baggage were everywhere. All the drawers had been pulled out and the furniture itself overturned. The room's personal safe was still locked and closed, but someone had a rushed crack at trying to pry it open, probably with a hefty Phillips screwdriver judging from the scratches. However much time they spent with the safe would have proved disappointing. Alexandra hadn't bothered to store anything inside.

"Oh my God, I've been ransacked!" Alexandra declared with amazement. She thought it only happened in the movies. Somehow she always imagined that if she experienced a break-in, the intruders would be a little more tidy. Surely, she thought, if you're searching for valuables, a careful, systematic approach would yield better results. Going out of your way to make a mess seemed counterproductive to an organized problem solver like Alexandra.

Nevertheless, her personal feelings on the subject didn't stop Alexandra from making an even bigger mess as she rifled through her scattered possessions and pushed around furniture to look behind individual pieces for the only thing she truly valued.

"It's okay, really. I can sign those papers later," Sid said, seeing Alexandra was occupied.

Alexandra ignored him and kept hunting, growing more and more frantic. Only when she picked up a final overturned dresser drawer off the floor did she find what she was looking for. Sabrina lay crouched and cowering beneath it. The cat bellowed a meow at her owner as soon as she was discovered. Alexandra scooped her up in her arms.

"My sweet baby! Did they hurt you?"

Sabrina was still stressed out from the raid, and being hugged close to a human didn't calm her down any. It had a soothing effect on Alexandra, however, who was instantly relieved that her cat had escaped injury.

"What were they looking for?" Sid wanted to know.

"The same thing we're looking for."

"Well it's not an animal," said Sid, giving Sabrina a friendly scratch behind the ear. "That leaves vegetable or mineral."

Alexandra sighed and reluctantly levelled with Sid.

"It's a recording of Helen sharing an intimate moment with a close confidante."

Sid nodded knowingly. "Fucking. Got it." Then he asked, "Format?"

"It's been immortalized on VHS."

"Video?" Sid asked with notable incredulity. "Haven't you people heard of the digital revolution?"

"This was an early production in the St. Simone filmography," Alexandra explained. "Strictly amateur, very personal, not for release."

"Well, let's be glad it's not in an upload-friendly format yet or kids in Singapore would be beating off to it already."

It bought them time, but not much. Any videotape was one video-capture card away from being dragged into the digital era. It was a fairly specialized piece of equipment, far from standard since tape was a dinosaur no one wanted to be bothered with anymore.

But for a Helen St. Simone sex tape, calls would be made, one would be dug up, and the transfer would get done sooner rather than later.

"We need to get you out of here," said Sid. "They could come back any minute."

"That sounds a bit over-dramatic, don't you think?" Trashed or not, Alexandra wasn't eager to leave her cozy, expensive suite behind.

"They didn't get what they were looking for, but they think it might still be here," said Sid, pointing out the damaged but unbreached safe. "Do you really want to hang around to greet them when they come back with blowtorches?"

Alexandra didn't have to think about it for more than a second.

"I'll start packing," she said, and began doing so at a remarkably rapid pace.

Sid sped up the process, helping Alexandra gather her assorted possessions, draping various articles of clothing over his arm. While he did this, he probed for more potentially helpful details.

"The tape was stolen from the house?"

"Yes," said Alexandra, "By Helen's personal assistant, Cynthia Gauthier. She's our murder victim."

Sid was thrown by Alexandra's horrible pronunciation. He'd been in town long enough to hear all the francophone names spoken correctly many times and made a best guess as to what she was aiming for.

"Is that 'Goat ire' or 'Gauthier?'"

"The French version," said Alexandra, not attempting it again.

"Where was it, exactly?"

"Hidden in an empty video box for the movie Dumbo."

"How'd she know it was there?"

Sid dipped into the bathroom to scoop up Alexandra's toiletries. He wrapped them in the largest, plushest towels he could find, whether they were wet or not, and slung the bundle over his shoulder.

"Everyone knew it was there," explained Alexandra. "About eight or nine years ago the house cleaner couldn't find a sitter, so she brought her kids over. She wanted to keep them amused for a couple of hours while she was working, so she sat them in front of the TV and popped in what she thought was a tape of Dumbo."

"How'd that work out?" Sid called from the bathroom.

"They were amused for a couple of hours."

Sid marched to the remains of the suite door and stuck his head out, looking up and down the corridor for any signs of life. Alexandra pointed at the bundle on his back.

"Those towels aren't mine," she told him, sure that the large hotel logo should have made that obvious.

"I know," said Sid. "They're mine now."

Sid spotted a bellhop pushing his newly unloaded bellman cart down an intersecting hall and called him over. As soon as the bellhop arrived, Sid started handing him Alexandra's bags, each of them hastily buckled and latched with clothes sticking out every side.

"Run these down to the lobby and call us a cab," he told the bellhop. "We're checking out in five minutes."

Sid held up a hand with all five fingers spaced for emphasis, just in case there was a language issue. He hadn't heard the bellhop speak, so there was no telling what his mother tongue was, and he wasn't waiting around to find out.

Sid caught the bellhop eyeballing the destruction in the suite. "And send a maid to take care of this mess. What sort of hotel are you guys running here anyway? Look at this shit!"

While the bellhop hurried to load his cart with all the refuse Sid was thrusting upon him, Alexandra stuffed Sabrina into her cat carrier. She was the most willing to get in that Alexandra had ever seen without her being heavily drugged. Apparently Sabrina had decided that since the cage smelled like home, it was the safest place to hide after the invasion she'd just suffered through.

Sid collected the cat carrier and shoved this final bulky item into the bellhop's arms before slamming the door in his face.

"Take a quick look around," Sid told Alexandra when they were alone again. "Whatever you want goes with us now because we're not coming back here for anything."

"Sid, half my clothes are still on the floor," said Alexandra, taking inventory of her possessions that remained flung to all corners of the room.

"What, you want all of them?" He had already packed more clothes than he'd owned in his entire adult life, and all the bags were on their way to the lobby.

▶ ▶ ▌

It took less than five minutes for the requested maid to arrive at the honeymoon suite, witness the aftermath that appeared to be the result of a tornado, and sink into an abyss of despair. By that time, Sid and Alexandra were already outside with the bellhop, packing bags into the trunk of a cab. The bellhop was trying to do a tidy job of it, but Sid kept throwing random armfuls of items into the back, starting with the last pile he'd wrapped up in a bed sheet along with a few more pieces of linen that struck his fancy.

Sid, at least, was satisfied that they'd salvaged everything of importance, but Alexandra was sure she'd be discovering orphaned shoes and missing accessories for many days to come.

Sid slammed the trunk shut, leaving a single sleeve dangling out over the bumper, and escorted Alexandra to the rear seat. He gave the driver an address that was an indecipherable French name, preceded by a mouthful of French numbers, also indecipherable. The cab pulled away from the hotel and headed, as far as Alexandra could guess, east. She had no idea where she was going but was satisfied that Sid was falling into his role as her own personal Sherpa, even with no down payment in evidence. Now that she had her guide, it seemed only wise to let him find her a path to safety. She figured there would be plenty of time to regret it later. For now, she was happy to let false hope have its way with her.

"So who's on the tape?" asked Sid, resuming his line of questioning once they were through the first traffic light and on their way.

"Just Helen and her ex."

Sid dug into his memory bank of Hollywood couplings. "Ben Rothstein?"

"No. Josh Fisher," said Alexandra, going even farther back into the roster.

"That's a lot of exes ago."

"Six boyfriends and three husbands," Alexandra summed up, skipping the flings and the one-night-stands. She had no accurate count for those.

"Time flies," lamented Sid.

Josh had been the love of Helen's life back before her life became public property. Then it all ended abruptly in a hail of tabloid speculation and public arguments. Deflecting blame for the power-couple's split had been Alexandra's first major spin assignment as Helen's newly acquired publicist. She'd spent an intense three weeks trading salvos with the Fisher camp until a child-star overdose swung the media spotlight away from the bickering exes. The upshot was twenty days of free publicity with fans evenly divided as to who was at fault. It was the perfect outcome for a nasty breakup and secured Alexandra a long-term contract. By the time the tabloids spilled more ink on Helen and Josh, they were both safely ensconced in new relationships that were fuelling new speculation.

"Does the next Mr. St. Simone know about this lost performance from his fiancée's archives?" Sid asked.

"I'm guessing not," said Alexandra. "And the less he knows, the better. Let's not hand him any ammo for the next divorce."

By all accounts, Nick Hadford was a nice enough guy, but he had his fair share of divorces and crash-and-burn celebrity romances to his name. Whatever he and Helen saw in each other, it wouldn't last to the end of the decade. Hopefully their trial separation, whenever it came, would stick and lead to an uncomplicated divorce, with all parties and lawyers adhering to the terms of the voluminous pre-nup. Alexandra just hoped Helen would ease up on the joint financial entanglements and adopted third-world orphans this time. It was a pain in everybody's ass to undo it all post-split.

"Is there anything illegal on the tape?"

"What do you mean?"

"You know. The usual. Livestock, minors?"

"No. Like I said, just the two of them. Consenting adults."

"Illicit drug use?"

"It wouldn't surprise me to learn they'd smoked a joint before rolling tape, but nothing that appears on camera."

"Anything kinky?" was Sid's next question.

"Kinky isn't illegal," Alexandra reminded him.

"Is that a yes?"

"It's a no. Why do you ask?"

"I'm nosy," declared Sid.

Alexandra knew it was more than that, and Sid was right to ask. Any sex tape was likely to alienate middle America, but other parts of the country might be more accepting. Unless the sex was weird. The open-minded demographic would drop off quickly depending on the fetish. Whips and chains were somewhat fashionable, but even the most libertine communities would turn their backs on someone who had engaged in, for instance, coprophilia. Luckily, the tape was from Helen's early Hollywood days, so the sex was fairly banal by porn standards.

Sid did some calculations in his head. There were no numbers involved, but weighing the consequences of scandal was more complicated than many advanced maths.

"So if this gets out…" he said, thinking aloud.

Alexandra interrupted him. "It can never get out." She wanted that to be clear.

"If," Sid emphasized. "Do we have plausible deniability? Can you tell it's her on the tape?"

"Sort of," was the best answer Alexandra's could offer. "The resolution's not great."

"Are there any close-ups of her face?"

"Just during the cum shot."

Sid was afraid of that.

"Our deniability just became implausible," he said. "At least we can count on TMZ not running any stills from that particular star-making moment."

The mainstream media would shy away from that sort of thing, even as their commentators chortled on-air and in print about the rest of the contents of the tape. Late-night comedy monologues and skits might suggest something more specific about the denouement, but would still have Standards and Practices to rein them in. The internet was another story. It would be linked to and emailed and blogged about and seeded around the world. Trolls on feedback forums would turn it into an animated GIF and use it as a signature. It would be absolutely everywhere. People would see it, even if they were actively avoiding it. If there was footage of one of the most famous faces of stage and screen getting spunked on, it would get around. There were isolated tribes in the Amazon rain forest who had never heard of electricity, let along Helen St. Simone, who would see it. They'd probably each get their own novelty T-shirt of the moment through trade and barter, and wear it around the village with their Nike knockoffs.

Alexandra looked out the window of the cab and suddenly noticed the neighbourhood had gotten a lot seedier since her five-star hotel.

"Sid, where the hell are we going?"

"Someplace nobody's going to come looking for you."

"Are you sure?" Alexandra didn't want to downgrade her accommodations from luxury to shithole unless Sid was certain.

"I've been there ten years and no one's come looking for me."

▶ ▶❘

Alexandra felt like a refugee standing on the curb next to the pile of her poorly packed possessions. She had little concept of where in the city she was. All she knew for sure was that it was urban, residential, and east.

Sid was already scaling a curving staircase of wrought iron and wood to his second-floor apartment balcony. The stairs looked like they would be precarious in a dry summer. Wet and icy, they seemed treacherous. He carried Sabrina's cage with him, which worried Alexandra, but he looked sure-footed as he pulled himself up by the railing, navigating a flight so steep it wasn't far off from qualifying as a ladder.

"This is it," Sid called back at Alexandra, "home sweet home. Grab some of that crap and come on up."

Alexandra looked around at the collection of two-level apartments that made up the area. They were all pressed up against each other, making solid rows that stretched from one street corner to the next. The buildings were nearly uniform, all of them dating back to early last century, thrown up en masse during a forgotten housing boom. Today, the neighbourhood was very French and, Alexandra decided, safely anonymous. She gathered her bags and started the arduous journey up the stairs.

By the time Alexandra arrived on the rickety upstairs balcony, Sid had his door unlocked. She followed him, stepping into the flat, struggling to carry all her heavy luggage at once. Once in, she dropped the bags, more out of dismay than exhaustion. Furniture was tipped over, broken, or both. Drawers had been pulled out and dumped, closets were empty, clothes were scattered everywhere. There was so much stuff tossed haphazardly around the place, there were hardly more than a few square feet of exposed floor in the whole apartment.

"Oh my God, you've been ransacked!" Alexandra gasped. Her mind was racing, trying to figure out how her next move had been anticipated, how her personal looters and pillagers had beat her to her next destination before even she herself knew what it was.

Alexandra was ready to admit defeat in the face of the criminal masterminds she was up against when Sid, completely unperturbed by the state of his home, tossed his keys into an empty pizza box sitting on a crooked end table.

"Nah," he told her, "I'm just not much for house-keeping."

The state of Sid's home looked like it should have been accompanied by an official declaration posted by the municipality, condemning the property. Alexandra was sure if she looked around she would probably find a biohazard notice and other reasons why the place was unfit for human occupation.

Sid stomped his way through the mess and Alexandra tried to follow, searching for solid footholds that would allow her the safest and most sanitary passage.

"How can anyone live like this?" she asked in amazement.

"Beats me," said Sid. "Better check my pulse."

"Seriously, did a bomb go off in here?"

"I don't entertain much. If I'd known you were coming to crash, I might have done a load of laundry and tidied up a bit."

Sid set down the cat carrier in a living room that looked like it couldn't possibly sustain life. Sabrina peeked out at her new surroundings from behind the bars of her cage and spotted something looking back at her from under a tattered recliner. She hissed at the creature, hair on end.

Alexandra bent down to take a look and saw the mangiest pitch-black stray anyone had ever allowed into their home. It glared back at her, deciding which instinct—fight or flight—would win out.

"Does your kitty play well with others?" she asked.

"Better than yours by the look of things," replied Sid.

Sabrina was making unnerving growling noises to warn off the other animal.

"Tell me his name isn't Mr. Whiskers," he commented.

"That would be Miss, actually."

"Miss Whiskers?"

"Sabrina," Alexandra told him. "Like the movie."

"You name your pets after movies," sighed Sid. "How Hollywood."

Had she actually been making the introduction in Hollywood, Alexandra would have been quick to point out that her cat was named for the Billy Wilder original, not the lacking remake from many years later. Here, she didn't bother to make the distinction. She assumed, correctly, that Sid wouldn't give a shit.

"That's Hoagy," said Sid, nodding at his own cat.

"As in Hoagy Carmichael?" she guessed.

"No, as in hero sandwich. I name my pets after food."

Sid gave Alexandra a very brief tour—one that didn't require them to go climbing over his collection of junk. He simply pointed out a goldfish in a bowl and a potted plant, both in the same room with them.

"That's my fish, Sushi. This is my fern, Cookie Dough."

"Plants aren't pets," Alexandra mentioned.

Sid put a finger to his lips. "Shhh! You'll give him a complex."

Alexandra unlatched the cage door of the cat carrier and tried to coax Sabrina out.

"It's okay, honey," she told her, "you're safe here. Come out and say hello."

Sabrina hissed again and then darted out of the carrier. She and Hoagy exchanged a quick back-arching confrontation and then chased each other out of sight under the furniture.

"I'm sure they'll work out their issues in time," said Sid.

Alexandra sighed, resigned to letting the cat power-struggle play itself out. She tried to kid herself that Hoagy was a full-time indoor cat who'd had all the appropriate shots and vaccinations. Her options for accommodations off the radar were nil, and worrying about what germs Sid or his cat might pass on to their house guests wasn't going to help matters one bit.

"The bathroom is where?" Alexandra asked.

"Through there, second door," directed Sid. "Why?"

"I just need to freshen up."

Alexandra had showered that morning, but five minutes in Sid's apartment and she already felt grubby.

"Probably not the best place for that," Sid called after her.

Alexandra turned on the light in the bathroom and saw why. There were tomato plants growing in about two feet of garden soil in the bathtub. The plants were each tied to a stick stuck in the earth, keeping them upright. The tap was left at a steady drip, either intentionally or through poor maintenance, keeping the roots perpetually moist and healthy. The tomatoes themselves were plump and red, getting plenty of afternoon sun through the dirty window. There was too much dust on the glass to allow a clear view out, but the light coming in was enough to permit the crop to thrive.

Alexandra didn't know what to make of it. Sid joined her in the doorway and looked like a proud parent.

"Hell of a ring around the tub you have there," she commented. "When was the last time you cleaned it out?"

Sid ignored the sarcasm. "You like? These are my babies."

Sid picked one of the tomatoes and bit into it. Juice squirted out of the ripe fruit, spraying the tiled wall.

"Mmm. It's harvest time," Sid declared, satisfied with his year's bounty.

"Where do you bathe?" Alexandra asked.

"Bathe?"

"Wash yourself. You're familiar with the concept?"

"The sink," Sid told her.

Alexandra looked at the bathroom sink. There was more top soil in it, with a different crop of half a dozen single sprouts poking above the surface, growing from the pungent edible bulbs below.

"The kitchen sink," Sid clarified. "But if you fancy a fresh onion…"

▶ ▶▍

Alexandra fancied neither a fresh onion nor a fresh tomato for dinner. The rest of what Sid had on hand no longer qualified as food, if it ever did. She was afraid to attempt to identify anything in the fridge, which better resembled a giant petri dish experiment run amuck. There were a few cans of tuna that looked fine, but that was earmarked as cat food. Ultimately, an intimate dinner of beer and pizza delivery on a TV table was decided upon, after which a couple of more greasy boxes and several empty bottles were added to the landfill Sid lived with.

Sabrina and Hoagy eyed each other suspiciously from opposite ends of the room, flicking their tails back and forth in paranoid agitation. So far, the territorial dispute was stuck at a draw.

The conversation had dried up and Sid looked lost in thought as he chewed on his veggie special. Alexandra sipped her beer, feeling a bit buzzed on the extra percent or two of alcohol above what she was used to back home. She tried to break the silence when she saw Sid was reaching the end of his pizza.

"So what do you…"

Sid held up a hand to stop her in mid-question.

"Digesting," he announced.

Sid washed his last bite down with a swig of beer and then thumped on his chest with his fist to bring up any residual gas. He belched silently, which was his version of being polite. Ready at last to articulate what was on his mind, Sid summed up his thoughts like a lawyer making a closing argument.

"So, disgruntled P.A. runs home to mommy in Montreal, only mommy never finds out she's in town. She's here for a whole day and there's no tearful re-union, no phone call, no nothing. Disgruntled P.A. never gets any farther than a crappy airport motel half a mile from the runway. And in that crappy airport motel she does six figures' worth of business with a hot property that's so hot, it gets her murdered."

"I don't understand it. Why Montreal?" Alexandra wondered aloud. "If she wasn't in any rush to go home to see family and friends, why run off to Montreal in the middle of the winter?"

"That's easy," Sid said. "The buyer was here. Montreal has the second largest porn industry on the continent, right after Los Angeles. L.A. was full of legal entanglements for someone who had just committed larceny, so Montreal was a no-brainer. It was a five-hour flight, she knew the turf, and she probably knew people who knew people who could set up a deal fast."

"But somebody didn't want to pay."

"So why write a cheque?" queried Sid, addressing his one sticking point in the story so far. "If you want to kill her for the tape, you kill her. What you don't do is invent some evidence and then try to burn it."

"So where do we start?" asked Alexandra, mindful that time was short and getting shorter.

Sid pondered this question a few moments and then sprang into action, rising from the not-quite-dearly-departed remains of his recliner and grabbing his coat.

"There's some people we need to talk to," he stated simply.

Alexandra offered him her cell phone. She had yet to see a working phone in Sid's possession.

"You need to make a call?"

"You don't call these people to warn them you're coming. Otherwise they won't still be there when you show up."

"These your contacts in low places?"

"No, they're higher up than the bottom feeders we're looking for. We'll aim low and work our way down from there."

Alexandra got up off the couch and joined Sid. She didn't like the sound of his plan, but it seemed right just the same. Despite herself, she was a little bit excited to be embarking on an excursion so far out of her usual realm of experience. Normally, she was all about the social climbing. This was like social spelunking.

"I guess I always wanted to know what it was like being a muckraker."

"This is what I call stepping into the shit," Sid told her. "Don't wear your good shoes."

Alexandra looked down at her fourth-favourite and third-most expensive pair of shoes and wondered how literally she should take Sid's words. She followed him to the door anyway.

"You two play nice," she told the antagonistic cats before shutting off the lights and leaving them peering at each other in the dark.

Montreal's red-light district had bled into every corner of the city almost as soon as it had accumulated enough burlesque venues and dirty-magazine shops to be able to call itself a red-light district at all. These days, it was even more spread out, with the smut sprinkled here and there all over town, often in otherwise mainstream commercial districts. The great intersection of sleaze that had permeated the corners of Saint Laurent and Saint Catherine was all but gone now. Urban renewal had taken its toll, and the area was now reduced to a couple of sex shops and one transvestite strip joint. And they were slowly losing their grip as well, facing the wrecking ball that wanted to turn them into part of a proper theatre district. It had been years since an undiscerning john could pick up a hooker outside one of the burger joints at any time of the day or night. Like every other creep, pervert or degenerate, they had to travel farther afield to find their fun now. Mostly online.

Even with the passing of an era, Montreal still enjoyed the economic benefits of being an adult playground. With the legal drinking age set at eighteen, kids from south of the border still drove north for graduations, birthdays, and bachelor parties where everyone could get a legal drink and pair of tits shoved in their face. The big-name strip joints in the downtown core catered to that crowd, but they were miles away from where the cab let Sid and Alexandra off.

Saint Jacques Boulevard used to be the main drag into town from the West Island suburbs, but it had fallen on hard times in the decades since Highway 20 was constructed as the principal artery. The boulevard still flourished in its own shabby way, but the aging motels and newer fast-food eateries were as inviting as it got. Less easy on the eyes were the car dealerships, industrial offices, and supermarket parking lots. Come nightfall, there was little to recommend the area unless you were passing through at 3:00 a.m. and absolutely had to have a coffee and a donut. Or a blowjob.

A good chunk of Montreal's low-end sex industry had settled here after it was run out of the red-light proper. Street whores didn't peddle their wares as openly as they once did, but they were easily spotted by anyone looking to make a quick personal connection. If you had the foresight to call ahead, a rendez-rendezvous with an independent escort could be arranged in whichever motel room she was working out of that week. And if you just wanted to look and not touch—or not touch much—there were a few dives on the stripper circuit that would do in a pinch if you were too lazy to commute the rest of the way downtown, or simply looking to have a beer in the company of other men who wanted to be left the hell alone.

The particular peeler emporium Sid delivered Alexandra to was called Lounge Venus. She immediately decided it was a misnomer when she stepped inside and discovered a dirty but functional black-washed pit that didn't qualify as a lounge, and failed to bring any images of gods of classical antiquity to mind. The place was full regardless—middle-aged, middle-class working men, sitting alone or in small groups. There wasn't a single drunken teenager to be seen, which was half the reason the clientele came here. The other half of the reason was obvious. The beer was a buck less than elsewhere, and the chicken wings were downright cheap.

The flesh on display was only wallpaper. Most of the girls weren't quite so cute or quite so young as the ones to be ogled downtown. They danced indifferently to pop rock that was at least a generation removed from the charts. Each had their own personal collection of piercings and ink unartfully etched at tattoo parlours of ill repute or no repute whatsoever—every one of them its own lottery ticket in the hepatitis Powerball.

Alexandra had been to a few of the carnival-atmosphere strip clubs in Los Angeles and had always felt perfectly at ease in mixed groups or ladies-night-out excursions. It took her a few moments to realize why this particular fleshpot made her skin crawl. And then she suddenly became very aware that she was the only woman in the place wearing any amount of genuine clothing. It drew the eyes of the men much more readily than the background scenery that was letting it all hang out.

Sid showed Alexandra to a free table. She sat down, but he didn't join her.

"Enjoy the show, order a drink," he told her. "I'm going to go see what's what."

Sid waded away through the clusters of seated men who were only half watching the girl currently on stage. She was midway through peeling off a nun's habit which Alexandra was pretty certain was not authentic to any particular order, unless there was an Our Lady of the Latex Garter she was unaware of. Other girls in easily-removed slinky outfits were working the room, trying to drum up business doing private dances for individual customers. There were few takers. Most of the patrons had to budget themselves between drinks and dances, and drinks were winning out.

The waitresses who were on the floor serving those drinks were only distinguishable from the strippers by their trays and money belts. Alexandra tried to wave one or two of them over as they bustled around delivering beers and cocktails. Having no luck, she finally gave up and sat quietly, assaulted by loud music and disco lighting.

One of the strippers in a hot-pink slip covering an even hotter-pink bikini approached Alexandra and launched into a business transaction mode every bit as impersonal as if she were negotiating the purchase price of a stick of gum.

"You ordered a lap dance?" the girl asked.

"No," Alexandra told her.

"I'm it," the girl replied, as if she hadn't heard.

"I didn't order a lap dance," Alexandra insisted, smelling a hustle.

"This is table seven, isn't it?"

"I don't know what table number it is."

"Table seven's got a lap dance coming," the girl informed her, dropping her slip and promptly straddling Alexandra where she sat. The stripper began gyrating mechanically to the beat of the song currently blasting over the sound system, grinding into her.

"Legal contact only," the stripper told her, getting the small print out of the way. "Tits and ass are fine. Touch my v-jay-jay and I'll break your teeth."

"What the hell is a v-jay-jay?" asked Alexandra, not really wanting to know the answer.

"Oprah-speak for a lady's baby-maker," said Sid, who had suddenly rematerialized out of the forest of gawkers. He sat down at the table and asked, "Don't you read O?"

"No," said Alexandra, "I just try to get people who aren't Oprah on the cover."

The stripper was now whipping her blonde extensions around in a wide arc as part of her dispassionate routine, repeatedly flogging Alexandra's lap in time with the music.

"Did you do this?" Alexandra asked Sid, cocking her head at the unwelcome interloper sitting on her.

"Not your type?"

"I'm not a lesbian."

"Neither am I," the stripper said, as she removed her bikini top inches away from Alexandra's face.

Alexandra turned her head to one side and hissed at Sid, "If I were a lesbian, I wouldn't be getting a lap dance in a tittie bar full of men."

"So where would you be getting your lap dances?"

Alexandra ran out of patience with Sid and his vulgar jest.

"Okay, we're done here, thank you very much."

Alexandra tried to push the girl off, but the stripper wouldn't budge. She clenched her thighs around Alexandra's legs and hung on tight, never interrupting her routine. A mechanical bull wouldn't have been able to buck her off.

"I'm sure you can find a more receptive vacant lap out there somewhere," pleaded Alexandra.

Men at the neighbouring tables were starting to turn their attention to the girl-on-girl action, finding it more arousing than anything happening with the headliners. Alexandra was feeling an unusual rush of self-consciousness.

Embarrassment rising, she turned to Sid. "Can we just find your contact and get on with this?"

"She's sitting on you," Sid told her.

Alexandra stopped trying to extract herself from under the lap dancer.

"Cheryll, this is Alex. Alex, Cheryll," said Sid, rattling off the introductions. "Cheryll isn't allowed to talk unless she's working, so I put her to work. You owe me twenty bucks."

Alexandra tried to be more civil.

"Is shaking hands considered legal contact?" she asked, awkwardly offering her hand. Cheryll shook it, business-like, but the two women were only inches apart and it made for a very cramped formality.

"I helped Cheryll out with a stalker problem last year," said Sid, explaining the connection.

"I owe him one," said Cheryll.

"She owes me a bunch. Her last cheque bounced," Sid said to Alexandra, even though it was directed at Cheryll.

"Money's tight. I have to prioritize," said Cheryll, talking back at Sid through Alexandra.

"Cheryll also moonlights as a performer in the occasional adult film."

"And I took calls for a phone-sex service one summer," Cheryll added, filling out her curriculum vitae.

"She's a sex-industry triple threat," Alexandra agreed.

"She knows a lot of the people we need to see," said Sid. He then asked Cheryll, "When was the last time you shot something with the local players?"

"Shit, those gigs have all dried up," bemoaned Cheryll. "I haven't fucked on film in ages."

"I thought porno was economy-proof."

"Hell, yeah," agreed Cheryll. "Nobody stops pulling their pud just 'cuz they're broke."

"So what's the deal?" Sid asked.

"Agencies have been dividing up the fur pie. You can't crack the door or spread your legs without representation anymore."

Sid had heard about the ten-percenters worming their way into the business. The days of porn being too seedy and distasteful for the usual film-industry handlers were over. Agents, managers and lawyers were snatching up performers for their stables of talent and cutting deals on their behalf with production companies. Back when the business catered to specialty theatres and the trench-coat crowd, these same people wouldn't have touched even straight-sex vanilla-porn. Now that the whole industry had gone mainstream, none of them were the least bit shy to call every sleaze merchant in town to push their clients and their specialties. Selling points like bukkake, salad tossing and cream pies rolled off their tongues, and suddenly nobody was squeamish anymore. The sex was dirtier than ever, but the money was legit. Even the pimps and the mob had been forced out to shadier pastures. It was the end of an era, and the days of some new piece of meat stepping off the bus in the big city and landing on a quality porn set as a solo act were over. Now even the most kinky carnal acts had a staff of wheelers and dealers shuffling legalese behind the scenes.

Sid still found it difficult to believe the paper pushers had sewn up the business that tight already.

"You're saying there's nothing out there for an attractive young lady with loose morals and a hot bod?"

"Oh sure," Cheryll clarified. "If I want to do bottom of the barrel ass-to-mouth scenes for peanuts, I can get work two or three times a week. But anything with any sort of production value? You need a mouthpiece working the angles for you, or you're locked out looking in."

Alexandra was having a hard time focusing on the conversation. Cheryll's laptop bump-and-grind was distracting enough, but feeling all the eyes on her was outright disconcerting. She finally turned to the men at the next table and snarled, "The show's on stage. This is a private dance, so fuck off!"

It seemed to do the trick. Eyes were averted, and the dance happening under the flood lights instantly appeared to have become fascinating once again. Sid smiled to himself, but refrained from comment.

"So why not sign with one?" Sid asked Cheryll.

Like everyone else in Hollywood, he'd always thought of agents as a necessary evil. Nobody quite knew what they did, but everybody knew they were essential.

"Who the hell wants to pay ten percent plus taxes? I want to get laid and paid with no paper trail. I didn't get into this line to give anybody a cut."

Sid nodded knowingly. Not so much because he agreed with Cheryll, but because he recognized her as the last of a dying breed. The under-the-table sex worker, soon to be as extinct as the dodo. It wouldn't be much longer before it was all regulated and taxed, represented and accounted, from the highest-paid adult-film actress to the lowliest streetwalker. He'd miss the sleaziness of it all and was glad there was still enough personal day-to-day sleaze in the world for him to carve out an off-the-books living.

For the next part of her oft-repeated routine, Cheryll hopped off Alexandra long enough to spin around and make a big production of bending over to pull down her bikini bottom. Alexandra turned her head away from the view. It was a little too close for comfort. She could see the five o'clock shadow on Cheryll's pubic mound.

"Okay, really, that's fine," Alexandra protested. "More talk, less gynecology."

"You miss it?" Sid asked Cheryll, indifferent to her current pose.

"It's better than stripping," said Cheryll after a scant moment's reflection. "Ever since all the clubs went contact, you can hardly do a table dance without some perv's hands all over your ass. You shoot a porn and at least you know you're getting touched by professionals who get regular STD screens."

"Who do you know who's still on the inside?"

"You remember Carlos?"

Sid sure did.

"You're kidding? Him? He's still around?"

"I see him every day," Cheryll told him.

"Lucky you," Sid said coldly, seeing no need to hide his contempt.

"Drop by tomorrow morning. I have a break around 10:30. I'll hook you up."

"He'll be there?"

"He's always fucking there," said Cheryll.

The current song ended, fading into the next track of unlistenable pop, this one only a decade out of date. Cheryll abruptly snatched her discarded garments off the floor and walked away.

"Where's she going?" Alexandra asked Sid.

"Sid only paid for one song's worth," Cheryll shot back over her shoulder, and disappeared into the dressing room to change into a new outfit, likely skimpier.

Sid got up to leave. He'd gotten all he could for one night.

"Don't look at me," he told Alexandra. "This is on your tab. That makes you the cheapskate."

Schooled

December 28th

ALEXANDRA SLEPT ON the couch, her body twisted into a question mark to avoid sleeping on exposed stuffing and lurking unruly springs. Sunshine flooded through the bent blinds and penetrated her sleep mask that had gone askew in the night. She pulled one eye flap down and tried to grab a few more minutes of rest, but the damage was done and she could sense unwelcome consciousness dragging her into a new day of who-knows-what.

Sabrina and Hoagy had stopping fighting long enough to have fallen asleep on the back of the couch at opposite ends. The warm sun didn't disturb them in the least. Rather, it only served to deepen their cat naps.

Sid strolled into the living room wearing a tattered bathrobe and nothing else. Pulling up the blinds, he let even more light in before approaching the couch and giving Alexandra's feet a quick tickle. It got her to tuck her legs in and leave him enough room to sit down next to her.

"What's up?" Alexandra asked, making no additional effort to appear awake or aware.

"Just thinking," Sid said wistfully, "It's been a long time since we woke up together."

"That happened once and once only."

"We were on a couch then too, as I remember." Sid ran his fingers over the stained and sun-washed fabric of his furniture.

"Couch?" Even half-asleep, Alexandra sounded indignant. "It was a hide-a-bed. What kind of girl do you think I am?"

"The kind that stays the whole night," Sid smiled at Alexandra, but she couldn't see it.

"I'd been drinking."

"It meant a lot to me. I liked making you breakfast."

"So what's stopping you now?"

He rose. "Eggs okay?"

"Cook them to death, would you?" Alexandra said. "I want to make sure you kill any germs they may have picked up in this dump."

Sid stalked off to the kitchen in pursuit of ingredients. Opening his fridge, he had a look at what was available. There wasn't much. He opened a carton of milk and sniffed at it to see if it was still good. The smell test was inconclusive, so he drank some straight from the carton to make sure.

Sid froze in place. The milk had turned. He took a moment to decide if it would be more disgusting

going down or coming back up. Bucking up his re-
solve, he committed to swallowing the mouthful,
solids and all, and poured the rest down the drain. It
came out in coagulated clumps which were zapped
with the garbage disposal until it was all gone. There
was another smaller carton inside, but it was cream.
Sid took it anyway and started to gulp it down, washing the taste out of his mouth.

Sabrina and Hoagy arrived at Sid's feet, meowing
hungrily and rubbing up against his bare legs. He
drizzled a puddle of cream onto the floor for the cats
to lick up and then took another swig for himself.

In the next room, Alexandra rose slowly, reaching
up under her mask to wipe the sand out of her eyes.

"What time is it?" she called out.

"Early," was Sid's response.

Alexandra groaned.

"Best time to get an early start," Sid added.

"I can't wait to see what slimy hellhole you drag
me to today," said Alexandra, not trying to conceal
her dread.

▶ ▶|

The campus was, Alexandra had to admit, quite
gorgeous despite the weather. The grounds could be
relied upon to look lovely in spring, summer and fall.
Winter too, but so far this one was not of the snowy
picture-postcard variety. There was cold, soggy mud
where the foot traffic passed, and frozen, solid mud

off the beaten path. Sid and Alexandra kept to the paved path, which was merely icy and dangerous.

"I wasn't expecting the halls of academia," said Alexandra. "I figured your contacts more for parolees who flunked out of trade school."

"I walk in many circles," Sid told her. "So do my contacts."

The university architecture was suitably austere. In the warmer months there was probably even ivy growing up the old stone walls. It was exactly the sort of school Alexandra's parents had longed to send her to. The only deal breaker would have been that it wasn't in America, and lacked the brand-name recognition of a Harvard or a Yale.

"You know, I could have made my mom and dad real proud by flunking out of a place like this."

"It's never too late to sign up for a night course and get an 'incomplete' for cutting class," Sid suggested.

Alexandra's family could well have afforded to send her to any school of her choice. A scholarship would only have been gravy if anyone passed her the gravy boat, but Alexandra never asked for it. Any of it. She felt her initial round of tuition money was better spent on a nice car. One semester of a business course in a community college later and she figured she knew everything, so she packed her closet into her still-new car and ran off to join the circus. That's when the real education began, cleaning out the cages of up-and-comers and down-and-outers in the

Hollywood zoo. No grades, no text books, no amount of tuition money could buy you that kind of learning experience. Most people couldn't make the grade. Alexandra passed, but not with flying colours. Even now, so many years later, she felt like suspension or outright expulsion was only one blown exam away.

Sid and Alexandra climbed the stone steps of one of the buildings and let themselves in. The main hall had a fair number of kids and hipsters milling about, but it was obvious the university was in the middle of its holiday break. During the semester, the same hall would have been brimming with students and stress, but between Christmas and New Year's the population was sparse and the mood relaxed. Any students still hanging around had successfully survived the first half of the school year and were yet to register for any courses, required or dreaded, for the second half.

Alexandra was so occupied studying the fresh young faces, still a degree or two away from having the hope and optimism crushed out of them, that she didn't notice one break away from the pack.

The unfamiliar girl excused herself to her friends and approached Sid and Alexandra. She spoke to them in a voice Alexandra was sure she'd heard somewhere before, recently.

"You're just in time," said the girl. "I have a study group in five minutes."

It took a moment for Alexandra to recognize who she was talking to. Daytime Cheryll looked like a bookish scholar, her tattoos and piercings safely tucked away under conservative clothes. They shook hands, which Alexandra found to be much more businesslike this time, when Cheryll wasn't inches away and naked.

"You clean up well," Alexandra told her.

"The whore-wear is a uniform. Same as if I were flipping burgers."

Higher learning may not have been for her, but Alexandra liked to encourage others.

"Good for you going back to school, trying to better yourself."

Cheryll's response was brimming with scorn.

"I'm not trying for a high-school equivalency here," she said. "I already have a degree in women's studies. I'm working on my post-grad thesis now."

"So what's stripping then," Alexandra wanted to know, "Research?"

"Tuition money."

"Women's studies, huh?" Alexandra sounded unconvinced. "I thought porn was the bane of feminism."

"That was the old days. Now we call it 'empowering.'"

Cheryll studied Alexandra's face to see if she was getting through to her. She wasn't. There always seemed to be a generation gap, right at a certain age that Cheryll was still trying to pinpoint. Thirty-eight and seven months perhaps? Further data needed to be analyzed. Regardless, she determined Alexandra was slightly too far north of the number, whatever it may be.

"You wouldn't understand if you've never done porn," she said.

"I guess not," Alexandra agreed.

The closest she ever got was flashing her boobs during Spring Break in Fort Lauderdale. There had been cameras in the crowd, and the moment was probably immortalized somewhere, but it was doubtful anyone would recognize her in those giant sunglasses. Still, Alexandra figured it was probably for the best that she never planned to run for public office.

Sid was ignoring the conversation, scanning the faces in the hall instead, keeping an eye out for one in particular.

"You sure Carlos is here today?" he asked. "The whole campus looks pretty barren."

"Everybody's home for the holidays except the ones who don't have a home or don't celebrate the holidays," Cheryll said.

"Which category is Carlos?"

"Probably both. He doesn't believe in much of anything, family least of all. I think he's sticking around to work on a film project."

"Is he still a shutterbug?"

Carlos had been very handy with his hand-held devices. His nimble fingers could snap any number of upshirts and downshirts in a matter of seconds without his subject being the slightest bit aware—at least until she recognized her bra or panties in one of the unofficial newsletters that clogged up the university email like a virus composed of malicious code and unsuspecting cheesecake shots.

"He's into movies now," said Cheryll. "Switched his major to film production and took a job shooting hardcore. It pads his résumé. He says he's a cinematographer, but he's really just the guy who holds the video camera."

"There's a difference?" asked Sid, not particularly caring.

"Cinematographers don't get hit with bodily fluids when they go in for a close-up."

Sid finally zeroed in on his target, arriving with a bunch of friends, in the middle of a heated discussion of no intellectual value. It sounded like they were debating sports, but nothing to do with the various varsity teams.

Carlos was only about twenty, but looked scuzzy enough for someone twice his age. Sid sprang into action and pulled out his digital camera, making sure he got off a few quick photos before he was spotted. He carefully framed his shots to make sure Cheryll was in the foreground and Carlos in the back. The autofocus did the heavy lifting.

Once Cheryll realized what Sid was doing, she gladly posed for the pictures, putting on a winning smile and running through the series of glamour poses she'd learned from fashion magazines back when she was a little girl and dreamed of being a clothed model. Sid's fast action proved to be unnecessary. Although Carlos was only twenty feet removed from the photo shoot, he remained oblivious to it until Sid called out to him.

"Hey Carlos!" Sid yelled, loud enough to grab the attention of everyone in the hall, "I'll have to get a measuring tape, but this doesn't look like fifty yards."

Sid wagged his finger back and forth, pointing out the general proximity of Carlos to Cheryll. Cheryll clarified the legal terms to Alexandra.

"I've been letting it slide," she said. "I got tired of narcing on him every time he broke the conditions of his restraining order."

"Wait, that's your stalker?" said Alexandra, realizing she was slow on the uptake today. She blamed it on a coffee-free morning.

"Yeah," replied Cheryll, "but he's eased up since I put Sid on his ass. Sid scares the living shit out of him."

Sid zoomed in on Carlos for a few closeups and got some quality candid stills of him doing an excellent cornered-rat impression.

"Smile!" Sid instructed.

Carlos didn't take his direction, opting instead to bolt as fast as his legs could carry him.

"Case in point," said Cheryll, nodding at the quickly receding figure of Carlos, who was already so far down the hall, he was nearly in the next building.

Sid cursed under his breath, saving his lung power for the chase. He should have guessed Carlos would be a runner. Sid hated runners. They only served to remind him how out of shape he was.

Without bothering to excuse himself to the ladies, Sid ran off after Carlos, attempting his nearest possible approximation of a sprint. Alexandra didn't have a stopwatch handy, but she could tell it took him considerably longer to make the length of the same hall Carlos had smoked in just a few seconds flat. Sid rounded the far corner and was gone. Alexandra could hear the squeak of rubber-soled shoes on the polished marble floors, and the report of heavy footfalls whenever the pair hit a straightaway. The sounds of pursuit quickly faded, with only the occasional loud door-slam or shout adding enough punctuation to the chase to announce that Sid was still in the race.

The racket finally diminished to nothing, and relative silence returned to the halls of the university. Only the white noise of casual student chatter broke the stillness. Alexandra and Cheryll stood quietly together in the hall, having failed to share the same sense of urgency that had set Sid dashing off into the maze of academic corridors. When it became obvious that Sid and Carlos would not be returning, Alexandra offered her goodbyes.

"Huh," she said, and then added, "Well."

"Yeah," agreed Cheryll. There didn't seem to be much more to add to the commentary.

"Thanks for introducing us to Carlos," said Alexandra. "I guess I'll go see how Sid's line of questioning is panning out."

Alexandra walked off down the corridor after Sid, in no particular rush to catch up.

Sid wished he smoked. It wouldn't have made the running any easier, but it would have given him an excuse to be this out of breath this quickly. With his otherwise pink and pristine lungs, he only had the fact that he was chasing someone half his age to excuse his poor showing, and he really didn't like to think about that depressing bit of math.

Carlos zigged and zagged down the halls, hugging his books and papers tight in order not to lose anything as he ran. Sid brought up the rear, trying to close the distance by cutting the corners more sharply than his quarry. Carlos would have lost him long ago, but he kept hitting doors that separated different buildings and departments, and it seemed like he was on the pull-side of all of them. Each of these doors was still yawning open after Carlos passed through, clearing the way for Sid and keeping him close.

Sid struggled to keep Carlos in sight. He didn't know the layout of the interconnected buildings, and one wrong turn would give Carlos all the advantage he needed to vanish. Carlos, however, wasn't trying to lead Sid further into the complex. He wanted out. There were still too many students around, acting as obstacles. Carlos was desperate to get onto the campus grounds where he could make a flat-out run for it. The grubby bastard behind him would never be able to keep pace then.

Carlos spotted the stairwell he was looking for. Only one more damn set of pull-open doors and half a flight of stairs lay between him and the exterior of the building. The final door beyond that was, mercifully, a pusher.

Sid rounded a corner, worried that Carlos had gotten too far ahead. He hadn't laid eyes on him in the last thirty seconds. Only the trail of disrupted students and a corridor that offered no branches had allowed him to keep the scent. Now it was the door to the stairwell, slowly swinging shut, that tipped Sid off to Carlos's path. Sid noted the red exit sign over the door and knew he'd lost his stalker target. The best he could hope for now was to see which way Carlos went as he disappeared into the city.

Mustering a final gasp of exertion, Sid jogged to the door, panting heavily. He slipped through just before it swung shut, and the first thing he noticed was that the exterior door, half a flight down, was still shut tight. No one had passed through it in the last few moments. Sid dreaded the notion that Carlos may had fled upstairs. He was sure any chase that took him more than one flight up would finish him off.

Sid needn't have worried, because he was heading downstairs whether he wanted to or not. Before he could reverse his trajectory, his forward momentum carried him right over Carlos's outstretched foot.

Carlos had been hiding behind the door, waiting to trip Sid and end the chase decisively. Sid stumbled forward as his legs were pulled out from under him. He spilled down the half flight of very hard stairs and landed at the bottom with a thud he was sure he'd still be feeling come the New Year. Before he could recover at all, Carlos ran down to the landing where Sid lay and gave him a good swift kick in the head. Luckily for Sid, Carlos liked his Keds, even in wet winter weather. If he'd been wearing boots or harder footwear, he might have knocked Sid's brains loose.

Content that Sid was in no condition to continue his pursuit, Carlos pushed through the exit doors and hurried to the safe haven outside. He thought he was away and free, but just before he hit the stone steps outside, a high-heeled pump suddenly jutted out from behind the door and tripped him exactly as he had done to Sid moments earlier. Carlos's books and papers went flying as he found himself tumbling end-over-end down a much longer, much harder flight than the one he had sent Sid down. It was a protracted drop with a lot of stairs, all of them stone. Carlos's initial scream was cut short by his grunts and groans until he came to rest in the muddy pathway below.

Carlos picked himself up slowly and saw Alexandra descending the stairs, heading towards him. He'd been badly pummelled, but was young enough to be able to walk it off—albeit with a pronounced limp. Frightened away all over again, he resumed his flight as fast as his injuries would allow. Alexandra made no effort to pick up where Sid left off. She wasn't about to chase anybody in heels. Instead, she turned her attention to Carlos's scattered papers that littered the stairs.

It took another full minute for Sid to drag himself to his feet and come spilling out the door. By then, Carlos had already made it to edge of the grounds and lost himself in the street traffic.

"Where is he?" Sid demanded, dazed but ready for a fight. "Where'd the little prick go?"

"Long gone," Alexandra informed him.

"You let him get away?"

Outflanking Carlos while Sid was futzing around inside was hardly letting him get away, but Alexandra didn't argue the point. Instead, she bent down to pick up one particular sheet of paper she had spotted.

"He didn't get away," she said. "I know exactly where he'll be and when."

Alexandra showed Sid the legal-sized sheet with a long list of names, occupations, times and locations. Sid squinted at it. He'd disassociated himself with the film industry too long ago to immediately recognize what he was looking it. He might have had better luck if his skull hadn't just had a run-in with a bunch of stairs and a Ked wielded with malicious intent.

"What's that?"

"A call sheet," said Alexandra. "Looks like Carlos is busy after school today."

The Lachine Canal had once been the only viable route for ships arriving from the Great Lakes. It cut a path from the midpoint of the island, all the way to the port of Montreal in the heart of the old city, avoiding a stretch of rapids that made other approaches difficult for small ships and impossible for large vessels. The days of the canal being the main commercial artery were long past, and now ships used the Saint Lawrence Seaway on the other side of the river to bring their cargo to town and beyond. The old canal had been preserved by Parks Canada as a heritage site, but token efforts to make it appealing for public recreation were limited to little more than a bike path and disconnected spots of green space. The carcasses of industrial-age factories still lined the waterway on both sides. One by one they were being refurbished as commercial space and condos. The buildings may have been ugly, but the bones were solid, and developers saw something in them worth preserving—hardwood floors and masonry mostly, certainly not aesthetics.

"This is the one," Sid declared.

He and Alexandra had passed a dozen ancient factories, some that stretched a whole city block, others that towered six storeys high, not even counting the disused smoke stacks. There was no indication of what was housed in any of them, but at last they had arrived at one red-brick and grey-concrete monstrosity that shared the same street and number as the address on the top of Carlos's call sheet.

Like most of the other buildings in the district, the former factory had been saved from the wrecking ball and converted for modern use. Now it was equipped with miles of new wiring and halogen lighting. The former manufacturing floors had been drywalled into dozens of individual units that could all be rented out at a premium, catering to companies that needed any size of workspace, from a glorified closet to a spacious loft. If it weren't all stuffed into such a hideous shell, it would look very slick and contemporary.

"It's a bit gentrified for porn, don't you think?" Alexandra commented.

"Porn is a bit gentrified for porn these days," said Sid.

Sid and Alexandra let themselves into the front lobby and consulted the tall glass case set in one wall that displayed a directory of the current occupants of the building.

Alexandra extrapolated some of the tenants based on their company names that ranged from clever to cryptic, "Website designers, search-engine optimizers, CGI animators, video-game networkers... It's like a mini Silicon Valley for tech startups."

Sid was already at the elevator—an early 20th-century design with new parts wherever needed to comply with contemporary safety regulations. He pulled the gate aside and Alexandra tore herself away from her directory perusal to join him inside.

"That's what scares me," he said. "If the tape is here, it's gone digital. And if it's gone digital, then it's everywhere."

Sid pulled the gate shut behind Alexandra and pushed the button for the third floor.

The corridor they stepped out into was just like the one on the main floor, minus any sort of open lobby. It was wide and ran from one end of the building to the other, capped by new windows that had been cut out of the exterior walls by the renovators. What used to be all open space was walled off with featureless whitewashed dividers. Set at regular intervals were a series of sleek and modern brushed-steel doors. The only way to distinguish one from the other were the numbers, although the residents of some of the offices had attempted to personalize their exterior with a company logo sticker or, in the case of the high rollers, simple embossed signs fixed to the wall.

The door Sid and Alexandra arrived at was one of the utterly nondescript ones. Only the suite number 305 indicated they were where the call sheet instructed its cast and crew to be. There was a buzzer to ring, which Sid skipped. He tried the door handle instead and found it unlocked. He and Alexandra poked their heads in and found it was one of the largest loft spaces, with a short hall leading to the open interior. They couldn't see anything around the corners ahead of them, but unconvincing gasps of "Oh, baby" and "Give it to me" suggested they had found the set they were after.

The film crew was skeletal compared to most movie sets, but populous compared to an average porno. Lighting, camera and sound were all separate jobs, and the set design, though modest, was thematic. Once the cast and director were factored in, the shoot was outright bustling with activity, and appeared lavish next to the typical fuckvids that filled the constant demand for new product.

Several other ready-made thematic sets were left standing on the ample floor space of the loft, ranging from atypical bedroom, to dungeon, to space-age science fiction. They were each in a state of flux, redressed and retrofitted to meet the demands of whatever sexual scenario was called for on any given day. Today, the main set was outfitted with a seasonal theme, complete with fake fireplace and a mantle with several Christmas stockings pinned in a row.

A pair of porn starlets were the focus of the stage lighting and hi-def video camera. They were dressed as Santa's little helpers, with green elf hats and not much else in the way of clothing. A third sported a pair of fuzzy antlers and what appeared to be a ball gag, modified to serve as Rudolph's red nose. Her sole job was to rub the nipples of the male lead as he worked his magic for the two helpers kneeling before him. The male performer was a hairy thug wearing a full Santa Claus suit with the pants pulled down around his booted ankles. Sweat trickled into his costume's white beard as he furiously built towards the money shot by his own hand.

The girls tried to look sexy rather than bored as they waited for the very literal climax of their scene. At the appropriate moment, a scripted line was delivered.

"Ho ho ho," stated Saint Nick, not so much holly or jolly as lecherous and lewd, "Santa's cummin' down your chimney early this year."

Alexandra didn't know where to put her eyes. This wryly amused Sid.

"You act like you've never seen porn before," he said to her.

"I've seen porn before," replied Alexandra. "I'm just not used to porn looking back at me."

Equally sweaty as his leading man was the director, though his perspiration came from lugging around his considerable weight rather than sexual exertion. He grunted as he pulled himself out of his director's chair—or at least what he thought of as a director's chair. It was actually an aluminum-framed deck chair that had been drafted into service when a short-sighted office-supply order had left the production mill short. Such staples tended to get overlooked in favour of prop furniture, like beds and couches and other viable sex-act surfaces. Crew seating was an afterthought at best.

Satisfied with his one-take wonder, the director called, "Cut!"

"Thank you, ladies," he added as a courtesy to the helper duo who had just finished their key roles in his latest feature film in thirty minutes flat.

"Do we have a towel for Tiffany?" he called out to no one in particular in his crew. Towels were also something in more ready supply than seating. One of the grips tossed some spare linen to the money shot's primary target so she could mop up.

"Was that a good one?" Santa asked his director expectantly.

The director had no patience for stroking the egos of temperamental performers. He cut straight to the practicalities of his schedule instead. "You got another pop shot for me? We can press on and shoot scene eight as well."

"Yeah, I can go again," Santa assured him. "I can't guarantee the same volume. Law of diminishing returns, you know how it is."

Santa's copious body hair was much darker than the bleached white of his fake beard, but he wasn't the young stud he once was. He knew it, and was always anxious to show he was still a workhorse, ready for another scene with a reliable erection at his beck and call.

The director turned to his cameraman and demanded, "Let's see the playback."

Carlos was the one equipped with the hi-def camera. He turned the display screen around so his director could inspect his handiwork.

"We've got it. Nicely framed, very artistic," Carlos boasted.

"Brightly lit and in focus is all I give a shit," said the director.

The crew bustled around, setting up for the next scene. No one paid any particular attention to Sid and Alexandra, least of all the performers, who were used to being unashamedly naked in front of all sorts of strangers. Sid and Alexandra both knew from experience that the key to infiltrating any film set is to look like you own all that you survey. Crews were always so busy that if they saw someone who wasn't schlepping, acting, or doing anything productive, they assumed they must be the backers come to check on their investment.

Sid and Alexandra waited patiently until Carlos happened to look their way. They both waved and smiled in exaggerated fashion, adding to Carlos's horror at seeing them in his workspace. His eyes darted around like he was considering running again, but there was nowhere to go on the job.

Carlos quickly finished screwing his camera rig to a tripod and slipped away from the setup to confront Sid and Alexandra in a voice as hushed and angry as he could manage without drawing attention.

"What the fuck are you doing here? Leave me alone, I'm nowhere near the crazy bitch!"

Sid took out his still camera and flipped through some of the pictures on his memory card.

"Not at this exact moment," he said. "But I have photographic evidence you were."

Sid hadn't sorted through the photos yet, but he soon found a candidate for personal favourite. Carlos and Cheryll were well framed and focused in the same shot. The look on Carlos's face was golden. He showed it to the stalker.

"Play nice or I'll email this to every judge with a hard-on for sex offenders."

"What do you want?" asked Carlos. Contrition at last.

"Just a meet and greet with your boss," Sid told him. "Tell him we're a couple of L.A.-based distributors come to see if we can cut a deal with…"

Sid trailed off, looking around at the facilities of the porn empire-in-the-making.

"What's the name of this outfit?"

"Poontang Posse," said Carlos, sounding vaguely embarrassed to even say the name out loud. It was hard to tell if he was more ashamed of the business or the bad alliteration. "Marty Guerin, he's the top guy."

Sid caught Carlos's nod towards the director and auteur of the holiday special that was shooting just in time to miss Christmas entirely.
"The director guy?"

"And the producer guy," Carlos added. "Owner, President and CEO guy, for that matter. He's pretty much the whole show."

Sid didn't doubt it. Most of the porn houses he'd heard of were one-man-bands, partnerships or, at most, a family affair. Cutting corners with office staff was a quick way to reduce the overhead, and the sleaze merchants usually preferred to push their own papers and count their own money.

"Right," said Sid. "Well, see if Monsieur Guerin is interested in cracking the southeast Asia market with his product. Go get him."

"And no more trouble with the law?" Carlos was hoping for some sort of assurance before he tried to rope his boss into a business deal he knew was bullshit.

"Keep your distance from Cheryll and the cops don't need to hear any more about your puppy-dog crush."

"I only took a few pictures for personal use," Carlos claimed, still fairly certain that his actions, though illegal, were morally ambiguous at worst.

"Through her bedroom window," Sid reminded him.

Alexandra appreciated Sid's performance as a man standing firmly on the high ground. She might have been convinced herself if she didn't know so much better.

"Don't worry about it, kid," she told Carlos. "Sid secretly identifies with you. Don't you Sid?"

While Sid spared Alexandra his best disapproving look, Carlos went to have a chat with his boss. The more Carlos talked, the more intrigued Guerin looked, until he finally came over to hear the pitch first hand.

"Mr. Guerin, I'm Sid Volke. This is my associate Alexis Meyerhardt."

Alexandra frowned at the introduction, but let Sid do the talking.

"What territories do you run?" Guerin wanted to know, ever eager to skip pleasantries when it came to professional matters. He considered such small talk to be on par with foreplay. Boring and unnecessary—something an easy flow of cash allowed you to take as read.

"Thailand, Vietnam, and a dozen Indian states," said Sid convincingly and with no hesitation. He had no idea what erotica distribution laws governed those places, but he gambled that Guerin didn't know either and hadn't done business with any of them.

"Not bad," said Guerin, who had only ever made sales in Japan.

"We're talking an extra billion potential customers who might enjoy a look at some pale pink flesh from the Great Whitebread North. Our market research tells us that a French Canadian accent exports well to some surprisingly diverse territories."

Alexandra chimed in, "It's sexy in any language, even if they don't understand a word."

The man in the Santa Claus suit butted into the middle of the conversation. Alexandra was relieved to see he'd pulled up his pants since last she saw him in action.

"Hey Marty," he said, "how long until the next shot? My agent wants to take a meeting now if I can squeeze it in."

Standing in the loft's doorway was a man who looked more like a banker than a sex-industry worker. He wore a suit and a tie—expensive ones. Too expensive to come from the wardrobe department, where cheap suits were kept on hand for businessman-fucks-secretary or travelling-salesman-fucks-bored-housewife scenes. Such a fine set of clothes had never been hastily stripped off and cast aside on the floor in the middle of a contrived sexual overture.

"And then he can squeeze me, huh? Fuckin' agents," spat Guerin. "This time next year you won't be able to pop a boner without letting them have a cut. Two inches off the top."

Sid didn't give the agent a second glance, but Alexandra gave him a good long look. The face didn't ring any bells, but there was something about the way he carried himself. Or perhaps, she admitted, she just had a taste for suits that ran four figures.

Guerin introduced his headliner to Sid and Alexandra. He figured the likelihood of them being star struck was minimal, but he always liked to show off the talent to potential business partners. At the very least, it assured them there were no open sores or needle tracks in evidence.

"This is Randy Dix," Guerin told them, "one of our regular male leads."

"That's Dicks with an 'x.' It's a stage name," Randy elaborated. He shook with Sid and then offered his hand to Alexandra. She left it hanging in front of her, untouched.

"Weren't you just masturbating with that?"

"Oh, yeah," said Randy, remembering his manners, and wiped it off on his Santa suit. He tried offering it again, but Alexandra still wouldn't take it.

"Pass," she said as politely as circumstances permitted.

"Dix in French means 'ten,'" Guerin explained to his new American associates. The pronunciation was different, but he skipped the nuance.

"As in ten inches," Randy winked.

"That way Randy's billing has cross-market appeal," added Guerin.

"Genius," replied Alexandra. She may not have spoken French, but she was fluent in her mother tongue of sarcasm.

"And that's coming from an expert," noted Sid. "She works in publicity. Hollywood big leagues."

"No shit?" asked Guerin.

"None whatsoever." It was the first thing Sid had said that wasn't.

While Sid wandered off with Marty Guerin to talk shop, Alexandra found herself being introduced to the suit at the door.

"This is my mouthpiece, Franklin," said Randy. He grabbed his agent's hand and pumped it enthusiastically, making the man wince.

"I thought I knew every agent in the business, at least by name. I'm blanking on yours," Alexandra told the suit.

"Tony Franklin," he elaborated, and offered her his hand once he'd successfully extracted it from Randy.

"Nope. Nothing," said Alexandra when her mental Rolodex came up empty. "But you look familiar. Did you hit any of the Oscar after-parties this year?"

Franklin smiled thinly. "I'm afraid not. There haven't been too many nominees from the adult end of the industry. Not yet at any rate."

"But someday soon, right?" asked Randy enthusiastically, looking to Franklin for assurance.

"Porn's going mainstream, you know," he added for Alexandra's benefit.

"I read the trades," she nodded, without commitment on the issue. So far, successful mainstream crossovers had been anecdotal exceptions. Whether more porn performers would manage it in the future was a matter of debate, although there was a time when it would have been considered impossible. That time was long gone.

On the other side of the loft, Guerin was giving Sid the grand tour of the facilities.

"So what do you think of our latest epic?"

"I think you missed the holiday rush," Sid told him. "Christmas came and went."

"St. Nick suits rent for a song after Boxing Day," explained Guerin. "We'll have DVDs of this holiday classic ready as stocking stuffers come next Christmas."

"It takes you a year to get a skin flick to market?" That sounded like a plausible post-production and distribution schedule for a real movie. But this was slap-dash pornography, more technologically advanced, but not that much higher up the food chain than the fly-by-night operations that used to make peep-show loops.

"Nah." Guerin confirmed. "We're just going to sit on this one until it's seasonal again. Normally turnaround is much faster than that."

"How much faster?" asked Sid, digging for specific numbers. "Say you got a really hot property you couldn't wait to cash in on. How soon could you get it on the shelves?"

"You're talking something in that can?"

"Yeah. Minimal editing, good to go."

Guerin was doing the math in his head.

"How hot?"

"Red," Sid said.

"Well, I have a sweet deal with a duplication mill two blocks over. I get them the masters and they can start mass producing within a day or two. Once they make delivery at the local smut distribution depot, the trucks can roll by the end of the week."

Sid tried to look pleased with what Guerin was telling him, but grave concern could still be read in his expression. He wondered how many other porn peddlers had a similar "sweet deal" that could mass produce on such short notice. He hoped the holiday stretch might gum up the gears and slow the whole process down just enough for him to play catch-up with the wayward tape. This hope was faint at best. No holiday was sacred enough to stop the wheels of commerce when there were this many dollar signs up for grabs.

Before Sid could dig any deeper into the Poontang Posse infrastructure, Guerin was distracted by the sight of Randy signing some documents for Franklin.

"Goddammit, do you have to stick that crap under my performers' noses when I'm shooting? That shit's worse than saltpeter for killing boners," Guerin bellowed at the agent. His indignity was forced. Randy's money shot had already been immortalized. Barring any additional lines of dialogue or reaction shots, his performance—the one that counted—was over. The next scene wouldn't shoot for another hour or two.

Franklin packed away the rest of his less-pressing paperwork. "Sorry, Marty. I didn't know you were rolling today. I'll come back to take care of business later."

"How much is this sack of meat gonna cost me now?" asked Guerin.

He was beginning to feel like a customer at a butcher shop where the owner kept weighing down the scale with his thumb.

"We're just doing our part to make sure adult entertainers put money aside for the future," assured Franklin, skipping any mention of his cut.

"I gotta think about my retirement. I can't keep this up forever," Randy agreed.

"This either," he added, grabbing his package under his Santa pants and giving it a tug.

As Franklin was closing the latches on his briefcase, Carlos saw an opening and slipped in with a question.

"Are you guys only representing adult film performers, or do you cover technicians as well?" he wanted to know.

"Just performers," confirmed Franklin. "But we may be expanding soon. And we're always willing to talk to exciting young talent."

"Talent? Hell, I got it all covered," said Carlos, going into his self-promotional pitch. "Tonsil shots, internals, you name it. Remember that M.P.'s mistress who did the porno with her blowing some Mohawk dude with a mule cock?"

"No," said Franklin.

Carlos was unfazed. "Yeah, well I shot the double-anal sequence on that. You ever try to pull focus on one of those? That shit takes talent."

Alexandra had taken a seat across the loft to observe Franklin from a distance. Randy came over to grab a bottle of water from the catering table and sat down heavily next to her.

"Phew. Tough day at the office," he announced.

"I'm sure," replied Alexandra. "It looks like you're digging ditches out there."

Randy had heard enough to start to take exception to Alexandra's tone.

"What do you mean?"

"It must be back-breaking, getting your knob polished by three girls at once and then cashing a cheque for it at the end of the day."

"Wait," said Randy, "you think I get off on this shit?"

"You're telling me you don't?"

"Nah," he replied, "doing this is just a job. It's hard work performing on command with all these people around. Don't let the hot chicks and skimpy outfits fool you. It's all smoke and mirrors and Viagra."

"So if all this doesn't do it for you, what does?"

"Gay porn," said Randy, sipping at his bottled water.

Alexandra nodded knowingly. She might have guessed.

At that moment, Marty was showing Sid into an adjoining control room that housed an impressive array of computers, monitors and sound boards. A pair of editors were already working with the raw footage that had just been shot only minutes earlier.

"This is my pride and joy," boasted Marty. "We can mix and cut on the fly. Raw material happens out there, finished product happens here. It's a modern miracle. Nothing like the old days when I was starting out and we had to get footage developed. We can show our stars what they look like in a rough cut before they even hit the showers."

"How much does a rig like this cost?" Sid wondered aloud, though he doubted Marty would be candid about his financials.

"It takes a toll, I won't lie," he said. "But it pays for itself. Eventually. Sales are up, so we can afford some shiny new toys."

As Sid wondered what other investments Marty might be willing to splurge on, Alexandra found herself sharing a heart-to-heart with Randy. It had only taken three minutes of casual conversation to lead to a confession about his rap sheet. Brought up without prompting, he spoke of it with regret, but it sounded like backhanded bragging.

"Yeah," the professional penis concluded, shaking his head sadly, "I don't think I was cut out for the gangs. Organized crime is a calling, and I just wasn't hearing it anymore."

"So, as mid-life crisis career changes go, how's this working out for you?" asked Alexandra in all seriousness.

"I like this business better," said Randy brightly. "There's not as much sex, but at least it's all legal."

"You two been getting acquainted?" said Sid, who had returned to check on Alexandra and her new industry friend.

"Intimately," reported Alexandra. "We've been sharing all our little secrets. For instance, Randy here will happily bottom for a scene, but going bareback will cost you double."

"Unless it's a real classy show," said Randy, offering up his one caveat. "Like a period piece set back before there were rubbers. Then you're just being true to the material."

"Keep artistic integrity alive," said Alexandra, as she and Randy raised their fists in solidarity.

Once she and Sid were relatively alone again, off to one side of the studio, Alexandra dared to ask, "Is it here?"

"Well, the Poontang Posse seems to have the cash flow to make a major purchase, but there's nothing that points to them as the buyer. You get anything?"

Alexandra nodded. "The agent who keeps looking my way."

Sid followed Alexandra's gaze and spotted Franklin and his briefcase heading for the door. He looked just in time to see him stealing another glance back at Alexandra.

"Maybe he wants to sign you," suggested Sid. "Or maybe he just noticed you checking out his ass."

"I've been checking out his elbow."

Franklin reached for the doorknob and winced again as he opened it. He instinctively switched hands with his briefcase, relieving his sore joint of the weight.

"There it is," Alexandra announced. "He didn't get that playing tennis."

"You sure he didn't get it jerking to the wares?" Sid suggested.

"I have a dent in my skull that says otherwise."

"Let's see if we can get a match," said Sid, and led Alexandra out into the hall.

They spied on Franklin from a distance as he boarded the elevator and shut the gate. Once the car began its descent, they hurried to the stairwell and ran down the steps to the lobby.

Sid and Alexandra avoided running into Franklin at the front door and opted for an emergency exit instead, but they were too late. By the time they got outside and spotted him again, he was already driving away from the parking lot in a luxury car that looked like it cost much more than what could be honestly earned skimming ten percent off porn performers.

Alexandra looked around for any means of following Franklin, but there were no other vehicles on the street.

"You'll never get a cab in this neighbourhood," warned Sid.

It wasn't that it was too dodgy, it was too industrial. Anyone who went there came in their own car or took a city bus. But even as he dismissed their prospects, Sid spotted Carlos standing in the front doorway having a cigarette break.

"You!" Sid shouted at him, loud enough for Carlos to drop his butt in alarm. "How did you get here?"

Confronted by Sid again, Carlos was immediately defensive.

"I drove," he stammered, almost apologetically.

"Good!" said Sid. "You're giving us a lift. Where are you parked?"

Sid grabbed Carlos by the shoulder of his coat and pulled him to the sidewalk, giving him a shove forward for good measure, insisting he lead the way. The trio skirted the edge of the building and stopped cold while Sid and Alexandra both stared in dismay.

"You drove here in that?" asked Alexandra.

Franklin rolled across one of the steel-framed draw-bridges that crisscrossed the canal. It was down—they were always down—locked in a permanent fixed position since there was never anything taller than a motor boat to let pass these days. As he headed north into St. Henri, the old industrial buildings fell away in favour of equally old housing that grew steadily nicer once he was on the other side of the train tracks. The gradual incline of the mountain marked the beginning of Westmount, and once he was above Sherbrooke street, the real-estate values abruptly skyrocketed. And still he rode north, up the steepening face of the western half of Mount Royal, towards where the city's skyline and money peaked.

All the way, he seemed unaware of his precarious tail. Hanging a good distance back were Sid, Alexandra and Carlos, all perched on Carlos's tiny scooter that was nowhere big enough for three, and barely sat one. Sid was doubled up on the narrow seat with Carlos, arms around the driver's waist. Alexandra sat back-wards on the stoop in the rear meant as a platform for small packages. She stuck her legs out the back, spread wide, giving the two wheels added balance to keep them all from tipping over into the middle of the traffic Carlos was weaving in and out of.

The scooter whined and protested as they pursued Franklin's car up one of the steep side streets that let onto the main artery of Upper Westmount. Alexandra saw the street name atop a stop sign on the corner. It was one of the few English-only signs she'd seen since she landed.

"The Boulevard," she read aloud. "Original name."

"You have to pronounce it *The* Boulevard," said Sid. "It doesn't need a name. All other boulevards pale by comparison."

Carlos turned onto the straight-and-level road that ran just a short walk down from the very highest point in town that wasn't part of the vast municipal park farther east. Opulent houses lined either side of the long stretch, all of them very British, very Anglo, very unilingually English. These were the heights the original local rich climbed to when Montreal stopped being a backwoods colonial fur-trading post and became a destination city in its own right. The money here was as old as the houses, and like so many wealthy neighbourhoods the world over, you'd never know anybody actually lived there. There was no one in sight, no signs of life in the houses, no pedestrians on the sidewalk. Just a thin but regular flow of traffic using The Boulevard as a quick and more scenic route from one end of town to the other. Winter and foul weather gave people a good excuse to remain indoors, but this seemed even more stoically monolithic than some of the richest districts of America Alexandra had seen. It was like a gated community without the gates. Perhaps the mountain, meagre as it was, was steep enough to keep the ruffians below from marching up for a look, for a piece of the pie that had been divided up generations ago, leaving only the crumbs to roll downhill.

Franklin at last pulled up to the curb outside one of the venerable grand houses. Unlike the collection of mansions all around it, this one was a hive of activity today. Several trucks were parked in the drive and on the edge of the property. A small army of caterers were patrolling back and forth, carrying folded tables, stacks of plates, and huge platters of hors d'oeuvres inside. While everyone else was buzzing around the house's side servant entrance, Franklin himself walked right up the main path to the front door and rang the bell.

Carlos pulled over, stopping nearly a full block away. Alexandra immediately hopped off from her uncomfortable perch and stretched out, digging her thumbs into her lower back and wincing.

"Ow. Ow," she announced for anyone who cared to listen. "Back, spine, ass. Ow!"

While Franklin waited for the door to be answered, he looked over his shoulder and surveyed the area, as though he were afraid someone might spot him.

"Back it up, back it up!" Sid barked.

Carlos cut the motor and they both shuffled their feet, edging the scooter backwards until the line of sight between them and Franklin was obscured by a row of hedges. Once they were safely concealed, Sid got off the scooter and dared to poke his head out from behind one of the old-growth maple trees at the side of The Boulevard that had stood there so long, the sidewalk had been specially cut to go around its deep roots.

Alexandra joined Sid behind the thick trunk and noted, "Nice crib. Think he lives here?"

"No," said Sid, "but his boss does."

When the door finally opened for him, Franklin reached into his briefcase to deliver a folder of paperwork. It was the same folder he had filed Randy Dix's contract into only twenty minutes earlier. The man accepting delivery was quite elderly, distinguished, and formally dressed in a manner that suggested someone who dressed formally every day as a matter of habit.

"You know him?" Alexandra asked.

"Nobody knows him," said Sid. "But know of him, yeah. Benton Manning. A muckymuck if ever there was one. You don't open a hospital or museum or cultural centre anywhere in this province or the next without a chunk of his change backing you up. He's the most famous low-profile rich guy in town. His face is always in the papers, but you never see it in person unless you're at least half as rich as he is. And that's richer than any of us mere mortals will ever know."

Franklin walked back down the path and drove away in his car. With their quarry departed, Carlos grew impatient.

"Can I go? I'll be lucky if I'm not fired by now."

"All right beat it," said Sid, approaching Carlos with a final warning. "Don't let me catch you nosing around the wrong girl's business again."

"What about those pictures?" said Carlos, pointing at the pocket where Sid had stashed his digital camera.

Sid produced the camera and navigated the menu. He turned the tiny screen towards Carlos so he could see and hit the same button repeatedly, running through all the most recent photos he had taken.

"Delete delete delete delete. Happy?"

"Thrilled," replied Carlos coldly, and started up his ride again.

The tiny scooter lurched forward. Carlos made sure to run over Sid's foot before U-turning into traffic and motoring away down The Boulevard and out of reach.

"Arg!" growled Sid. "Motherfuck!"

Alexandra ignored Sid's pain and walked over to the nearest catering van. She looked at all the food in the back that was yet to be unloaded.

"I wonder who the party's for," she commented. "And when."

Sid limped over and scooped up some icing from the edge of a huge cake that was resting on the edge, earmarked to be ported inside next. He taste-tested it off the end of his finger and contemplated the sugary confection like a connoisseur.

"Tonight," he deduced. "This won't keep."

Some of the caterers were back outside, returning for another load. Sid and Alexandra walked away casually, like they were the lone pedestrians with the whole boulevard to themselves.

"Think maybe we should invite ourselves?" suggested Alexandra. "See who's trying to play pimp to every local skin flick?"

"Are you crazy?" said Sid. "They'll have security working the door. We won't get two steps onto the property before they have the dogs on us."

"You don't need an official invite to a formal party with the movers and shakers of this world," Alexandra informed Sid. "You just need to look like you can move and shake with the best of them."

▶ ▶❙

The kitchen sink was full of water, topped with a foamy film on the surface. Alexandra dipped a pink disposable razor in the water and shook it to wash off some more foam and stubble. She had Sid seated on a stool next to the counter with a table cloth tied around his neck. Her collection of personal toiletries was set out on the table and she was accomplishing what she could with what she had on hand. A clean shave was the top priority.

Alexandra scraped another row of whiskers off of Sid's lathered face and returned to the sink. While her back was turned, he became interested in a can of body spray that towered in the centre of the jars and tubes on the table. He picked it up so he could read the label and spray some into the air. Sid sniffed at the cloud that hovered over him. It was the prettiest scent his apartment had hosted since he first moved in so many years earlier.

"This smells nice," he said. "Very lady-like."

Sid sprayed a generous dose into one of the armpits of his shirt. Alexandra wrestled the spray can away from him.

"Don't touch my products," she commanded. "Ever."

Alexandra snapped the top back on and returned the spray to her collection.

"You know," Sid said, unfazed by the confiscation, "if you end up crashing here again tonight, you'll have stayed over at my place twice as many nights as you ever did back in the day."

Alexandra hunched over Sid with her razor, fine-tuning her grooming job. A number of extra-thick strands had survived the deforestation and were stubbornly refusing to come off without a fight.

"Desperate times, desperate measures," she said.

"That was what, ten years now? I thought we were hitting it off then, but you never said more than two words to me again."

"Yeah, well, have you looked in a mirror lately?"

"That was way before I let myself go. In those days I used to brush my teeth and scrub between my toes and everything."

Having been employed to shave her legs a few times now, Alexandra's disposable razor was begging to be disposed of. Unfortunately, it was the only one she had, and it lacked the kind of edge required to contend with Sid's bristles. She resorted to tweezers to pluck a final few saplings out of Sid's chin, making him wince each time.

"It was a conflict of interest, Sid. I build stars up. Your job was to tear them down."

The door buzzer rang, a loud and unpleasant noise left over from the building's original design when the technology of a simple "ding dong" eluded humanity.

"I'll get that," Alexandra said, trotting off. "You just sit there and try not to grow it all out again before I get back."

Sid poked at the clumps of fuzz on the floor with his toe. His hair was still wet from Alexandra giving him a trim on top as well. Some of the tangles had proven so resilient, it was easier to cut them away than attempt to untie them.

He grabbed his stainless-steel toaster, the only reflective surface available, and took a look at the damage. It was the most presentable he'd looked in years. Baring his teeth, Sid checked for trapped food, and then used the table cloth around his neck to wipe off the remains of the shaving cream.

Curious about what was keeping Alexandra at the door, he got up to see for himself and found her finishing a transaction with a courier, who was swiping her gold card in his reader. Alexandra signed for the garment bag delivery and shut the door.

"What's that?" asked Sid.

"It's your rental tux. Shirt, jacket, pants. Tell me you've at least got shoes and socks of your own that will go with this."

"I don't know. Check the laundry hamper."

Alexandra handed Sid the garment bag. He took it, even though he was uncertain whether he wanted it at all.

"Try it on," she said, and disappeared into Sid's bedroom. "I want to make sure it fits. I gave them best-guess measurements."

Alexandra found Sid's laundry hamper and opened the lid. The stench rose from the unwashed clothes like an uppercut and she immediately recoiled, gasping for air.

"Gah!" she exclaimed. "What do you keep in here, tear gas?"

"And my valuables," said Sid. "It's better than a safe and alarm system. Any burglar brave enough to go digging in there is welcome to rob me blind. He'll have earned it."

She threw the lid back on the hamper from a safe distance.

"I'll try my luck in the closet."

Alexandra opened the closet door and rifled through the contents. They were mostly empty hangers. It took her a few moments to notice the eyes that

were watching her from the corner, glowing in the
near dark of the interior.

She leapt out of the closet with a scream. Sid came
running into the room to see what was wrong.

"What the hell's that!" Alexandra screeched.

Something large and hairy came spilling out of the
closet and toddled across the room to hide under the
bed.

"That's my raccoon, Pork Chop," answered Sid,
relieved that was what all the fuss was about.

"You have a pet raccoon?" Alexandra asked as
she recovered her breath. She didn't really sound at
all surprised.

"I wouldn't exactly say 'pet.' He comes and goes
as he pleases. I think there's a hole in the roof."

"What's it doing in the closet?"

"Sleeping probably. He's nocturnal."

"Are there any other critters running around here
I should know about?"

Sid thought about it for a few moments.

"There's my mouse, Cheeseburger. He lives in the
walls. That's the last one, I think. Actually, as far as I
know, it could be fifty mice. But I only ever see one at
a time, so collectively they're called 'Cheeseburger.'"

Alexandra threw up her hands dismissively.
"Okay, I'm done rummaging around this sewer. I
don't know what I'm going to find next. A yeti or a
sasquatch probably. Find your own damn shoes and
socks, I'm going to go put on my face."

With that, she left Sid to do his own wardrobe hunting.

The hunt did not go well.

When Sid returned to the kitchen with his tuxedo on, he might have looked halfway respectable if not for the old sneakers with no socks. He caught Hoagy staring up at him, head cocked, not sure what to make of his master.

"What the hell are you looking at?" Sid demanded of his cat.

Hoagy decided he didn't care for what he was seeing, whatever it was. He arched his back, hissed once, and ran away.

Sid found Alexandra bent over the sink with her hair pinned back, rubbing some cream into her face. She'd had the same idea as Sid, and used the toaster as a mirror while she applied the facial cleanser.

"What beauty product is that now?" Sid asked, not really wanting to know the gory details.

"I'm exfoliating," explained Alexandra, knowing the word, the concept, was probably foreign to Sid.

"Maybe I need to exfoliate, too," Sid wondered aloud, reaching for the tube.

Alexandra slapped his hand away.

"I've done what I can for you with spit and polish. I'll make up the difference by being so fabulous, no one will bother to look at you."

Sid saw a bottle of mouthwash sitting on the kitchen counter and took the opportunity to cup his hands over his mouth and nose, breathing out through his mouth and back in through his nose. Sid's eyes teared up, flittering and rolling back in reaction to his own odour. When Alexandra closed her eyes to rinse cleanser off her face, Sid borrowed her mouthwash and sucked a swig straight out of the bottle. He swished the medicinal green liquid around in his puffed-out cheeks.

With her eyes still shut, Alexandra reached for a towel. Desperate not to be caught touching her stuff again, Sid looked around for a place to spit. Alexandra was blocking the sink, limiting his options, so he resorted to spitting the contents of his mouth back into the mouthwash bottle. He screwed the cap back on and returned it to the counter just in time to avoid notice. The interior of the bottle now sported a bubbly green head and a single Cheerio drifting to the bottom of the swill, but looked otherwise unmolested.

Alexandra took a glass out of the cupboard and inspected it for dirt.

"Has this been washed?" she asked.

"Oh, sure," claimed Sid, who was confident it must have been washed at least once in its life, just not by him and certainly not in years. At least it looked clean. Cleanish.

Alexandra poured herself a precise measure of mouthwash from the same bottle Sid had just defiled and tossed it back. She swilled the shot around and spit it into the sink. There was, perhaps, a moment where she detected an unfamiliar taste, but Sid distracted her before she could consciously question it.

"So do I clean up nice?"

Alexandra looked Sid up and down.

"You clean up...adequately," she concluded. "You're perfectly presentable. From a safe distance."

"And, might I observe, you're looking much less hideous yourself this evening," Sid mustered.

"You say the sweetest things. No wonder we're still together after all these years."

"I'm ready. Are you ready?"

Alexandra was still in her slip and underwear while she worked on her face.

"Do I look ready?"

To Sid, any clothes meant dressed, and dressed meant ready. He turned to Sabrina and Hoagy where they were perched, watching the party preparations closely.

"Okay, we're off," he told them. "Don't wait up."

Guests streamed into the Benton house at an orderly, languid pace. Everyone was dressed too sharply to risk a bottleneck at the front door that might leave somebody wrinkled or moistened, so they took their time making their way up the path once their drivers let them off. Each grand arrival gave them time to be seen, admired, and photographed by the local media that had been dispatched to cover the event, a charity fundraising dinner as it turned out.

Sid and Alexandra arrived by cab. Although many of the guests had personal chauffeurs or rented limos for the occasion, some of the less ostentatious guests also came by cab or drove themselves, so there was no undue attention directed at the infiltrators when they were let off at the curb.

Alexandra had opted for a sleek but simple evening gown, partly to avoid too many interested eyes, but mostly because that was the one that had best survived the hotel bugout to Sid's apartment without any major creases, tears or stains.

When it was their turn to traverse the catwalk path, the photographers turned their lenses on them as part of their social-event photo-op dragnet. Nobody in the media could have possibly recognized them, but better to waste a few shots on nobodies just in case they turned out to be somebody when the story was being edited for the morning news. Sid knew that ass-covering technique well from his days among the paparazzi. You never knew when some surprise big name might be flying under the radar, or when some nameless hanger-on might turn out to be the centre of an upcoming scandal.

Although there was security working the door, they were mostly concerned with keeping photographers off the lawn and making sure the one or two reporters waiting for specific politicians kept their ambush questions from getting too aggressive and spoiling anyone's appetite. Some of the guests made a token effort to flash their elaborate invitations, hand-printed on stylistically distressed parchment, to the closest hired hand at the entry. But most opted to simply nod politely, as though they should be instantly recognizable to any reputable security personnel who might be working such an evening. Alexandra, with Sid following her lead, offered her own familiar nod to the tuxedoed muscle at the door. The security looked right through them as though they weren't even there.

Once inside, they kept their pace slow and even and unsuspicious.

"Polite wave like you know someone," Alexandra instructed Sid in a low voice, raising a white-gloved hand to no one in particular.

"Pretend to make eye contact with the wall," she said, fixing on an imaginary acquaintance.

"Smile of recognition to no one in particular," she added, through teeth that were clenched in a fixed grin.

Sid mimed each of these gestures in mirror image to Alexandra as they passed through the front hall and into the mingling crowd beyond.

"And we're in," Alexandra announced, satisfied.

"You're a natural," Sid told her. "It's like bullshit is your first language."

"Years of practice," she said, collecting two cock-tails off a passing caterer's tray. "There's at least three must-crash parties in Hollywood every week."

"Think we can blend in and continue to go unno-
ticed?" Sid asked, accepting his delicate pink beverage
from Alexandra.

"I don't see why not. No one in this town knows
me, and no one would admit to knowing you."

Sid and Alexandra clinked their glasses together,
satisfied with their anonymity. As they both took a
sip, they were interrupted by a familiar voice that
nearly made them choke.

"Madame Middleton, Monsieur Volke, I am surprised to see you here together."

The double spit-take drew all sorts of unwanted
attention. Alexandra was barely able to keep her
composure enough to refrain from dribbling all over
herself. Sid maintained his composure, but let the
dribbling cocktail flow freely, forgetting he'd been
sheared of the catch-all beard that was his normal
safety net in such drink and food mishaps.

"But then again," continued Inspector Langelier,
"I am surprised to see either of you here at all."

"Oh, hey Bernard," said Sid, reacquainting himself
with someone whose acquaintance he would have
preferred to skip. "How are things hanging down at
the cop shop?"

"We miss you terribly. I have not seen you since
the acquittal."

"Suspended sentence, actually," Sid corrected him.

Sid clarified in the vaguest possible terms to Alexandra, "Minor misunderstanding over a point of law.
All in the line of duty."

"No doubt," said Alexandra.

"How do you two know each other?" Langelier inquired.

"Blind date," claimed Sid. "An internet match-making service said we were soul mates."

Inspector Langelier looked the couple up and down, comparing and contrasting with his trained eye.

"You should demand a refund."

"It seems we share the same taste in charity fund-raisers," said Sid. "So far, so good."

"Then you've met our hosts of course."

Langelier tapped an older gentlemen on the shoulder, drawing him away from his current station where he had stopped to make the rounds. Benton Manning turned around and deigned to say hello. His wife, tight on his arm, pivoted with him in their balletic dance of high-society glad-handing. They were a spry pair of senior citizens, and had been a dashing, affluent couple in the social scene for as long as anyone could remember.

"Benton, Louise," began Langelier, "may I present Mr. Sidney Volke and Ms. Alexandra Middleton. You're familiar with the Mannings, I'm sure."

It sounded like a test, but Benton Manning was not one to let an awkward introduction to complete strangers linger in the air for more than half a second. He took Sid's hand and shook it vigorously.

"Thank you so much for your support," he told Sid earnestly, genuinely, like a politician stumping for votes. Sid ran with it.

"Oh, of course," he said, shaking Benton's hand right back at him. "Such a worthy cause."

"So close to my heart," Alexandra assured the Mannings, holding her hand to her chest and beaming her best empathetic expression.

The moment the Mannings returned their attention to Langelier, Sid and Alexandra exchanged a quick shrug and frown. Neither of them had bothered to look into exactly what cause they were supposed to be supporting that night.

Langelier continued with his formal introduction.

"Ms. Middleton comes to us this evening from Los Angeles, where I understand she works with some of the biggest names in Hollywood."

"How glamorous," gushed Louise Manning, star struck. "Are you an actress?"

"Publicist."

"For anybody very famous?"

"Helen St. Simone," said Alexandra, deciding to drop the name and see if it got a reaction. It did.

"Oh, she's very good!" Louise declared. "Such a lovely girl, and so charitable, adopting those poor African refugees."

"I'll be sure to let her kids know," replied Alexandra politely, "next time I'm in Africa."

Helen preferred her children to arrive like all her other impulse buys—with a thirty-day return policy.

"Mr. Volke has been an asset to several of our department's investigations over the years," Langelier told their hosts. "He can also brag of many useful connections who are—well, shall we say—out of the mainstream."

"Scum," said Sid. "Bernard is talking about the scum I have to deal with on a daily basis as part of my job. But of course, Mr. Manning wouldn't know anything about the underbelly of this city. Just looking around, I can already tell I'm the lowliest lowlife here."

Sid looked directly at Benton Manning.

"Maybe second lowest," he concluded.

But Sid's attempt to bait Benton bounced off his target harmlessly.

"It's true," said Benton, "I walk in some pretty affluent circles. But all the better to raise money for those who are truly in need."

"You must tell me about some of these nefarious characters you know, Mr. Volke. I'm fascinated." said Louise, sounding almost as star struck by the mention of Sid's associates as she had been by Alexandra's.

Louise took Sid by the arm and led him off while her husband excused himself and went to mingle with his next group of patrons. Sid glanced back at Alexandra over his shoulder and tilted his head towards the rest of the house, silently instructing her to check it out on her own. Before she could slip away, however, Langelier stepped in front of her.

"I am glad to see you up and about after your trying experience, Madame Middleton."

His words were nice enough, his concern perhaps genuine, but he sounded suspicious just the same.

Alexandra chose to ignore the mention of her recent troubles and focus elsewhere.

"I love being called 'Madame.'" she said. "It makes me feel so exotic. Like the proprietress of a Nevada whorehouse."

Langelier only responded by sticking to business.

"Obviously, I cannot discuss an investigation in progress. But I did call your associates in Los Angeles to ask them about the late Cynthia Gauthier."

Alexandra tried to mask the troubled look she felt crossing her face.

"Oh, really?"

"They were rather evasive."

Alexandra looked relieved, but only for a moment.

"Until I told them she had been murdered," continued Langelier. "One young man sounded quite distressed. He mentioned there was property missing."

Alexandra could guess who blabbed.

"Jeffrey," she acknowledged through a false smile. "He's easily rattled."

"And you are not," Langelier said back at her through his own smile, equally false.

"Some home movies?" he asked, once the smiles became too forced. "Montreal seems a long way to travel to recover a—videotape, is it? Even one that belongs to a big celebrity like Helen St. Simone."

"I didn't come here looking for home movies."

"No, of course not," Langelier agreed. "Why would you? Unless there was something horribly compromising in this video. But I am just speculating, of course."

"Is that what police here do?" Alexandra asked him more pointedly. "Speculate? Make up stories if they can't find any evidence?"

"Sometimes it suggests to us what evidence we need to be looking for, Madame."

▶▶|

Sid looked at the length of the lavish buffet that was set out for the occasion in a dining room nearly big enough to qualify as a dining hall. It was all meat, fish and poultry. Any scraps of vegetable were there for decorative flair.

"Quite a spread," Sid commented.

"It's a night of gluttony for the wealthy," agreed Louise. "But it's all for a good cause."

"I'm sure the..." Sid began.

He took a blind guess at the cause, searching Louise's face for any hint that he was on the right track.

"Orphan...crack babies...will be very grateful."

"Homeless," said Louise.

Sid winced in pain, like a contestant who had just missed a quiz-show question.

"Don't worry, Mr. Volke," Louise assured him. "I can't keep track of all the charities myself. It's good of you to come, just the same. All this raises money for the new Cartier Bridge Mission. It's a shelter and soup kitchen."

"I could have guessed it wasn't an animal shelter," Sid said, looking at the buffet.

"Is that a criticism of the menu?" Louise asked. "You're not a vegan, are you?"

"No, I don't care if an animal made my food. Just so long as it's not made out of the animal itself."

"Vegetarian then," said Louise. "I've never really understood vegetarians. With so many mouths to feed in this world, we can hardly afford the luxury of being picky about what we eat. And how can anyone morally justify preserving the life of an animal over the life of a person?"

Sid considered Louise's words.

"Take the worst animal in the word," he said at last. "Say, some rabid, pissed-off Bengal Tiger with a thorn up his ass. He'd tear your throat out. But he'd never stab you in the back. And that's more than I can say about some of the best people this world has to offer."

A stranger, isolated and unknown by anyone in sight at last, Alexandra crept away, heading upstairs as quietly as she could, careful not to creak the stately wooden stairs above the din of the party below. One by one she opened the second-floor doors to look inside, searching for a room that looked promising.

Hearing footsteps coming up the stairs—ones not so measured and cautious as hers—Alexandra ducked into the nearest available room and swung the door nearly shut. She left it slightly ajar for fear that closing it might make too much noise and expose her. Through the gap, she saw it was Franklin who had ascended to the landing. She hadn't seen him arrive with the other guests, hadn't spotted him mingling. He might have been in the house before any of the others for all she knew—might have seen her and Sid hobnobbing with Manning and was now on the prowl for them.

Franklin walked down the hall, passing within a few feet of Alexandra, then stopped in mid-stride and returned to the room she was hiding in. Alexandra held her breath and hid in the darkness behind the door. She could see the shadow of Franklin's feet, cast under the door by the hall light, only inches away.

Alexandra kept holding her breath, though she wondered if the better idea might be to inhale deeply and blurt out an excuse for her intrusion, followed, perhaps, by another deep breath and a run for it. But Franklin didn't enter the room. He only shut the one door left ajar, leaving Alexandra standing in the pitch-black, before continuing down the hall.

Unwilling to eat most of what was on the menu, Sid had arrived at a compromise, piling a huge helping of mashed potatoes onto his plate, along with a few spare vegetable garnishes. He sat down at one of several rapidly filling tables in the dining room, next to a grand old-money dame he knew he should recognize if he only he kept better company. There was a re-served-seat card with a name printed on it at his place setting. Sid didn't read it, and stuffed it into the centre-piece, between the arrangement of fresh flowers, until it sank into the water at the bottom of the vase.

The lady next to him looked disapprovingly at Sid's heaping portions. She, herself, had opted for a modest cut of veal.

Sid began his meal by carving a deep trough in his potatoes and filling it with gravy from a boat that was making the rounds at the table. He then piled more mashed potatoes over the trough, burying the gravy core, and set to sculpting the off-white mush on his plate with a fork. The lady one seat over tried not to take notice of Sid playing with his food. She attempt-ed to avert her eyes, but couldn't help but steal an occasional glance at her neighbour's handiwork as it progressed, even as she tried to involve herself in polite conversation elsewhere.

The potato sculpture began to take on a definite, recognizable form, assuming the outline of a cute running bunny. Selected vegetable garnishes were pressed into service to highlight the features and bring the creation to life. A single pea formed the eye, a piece of cauliflower the fluffy tail, a bay leaf the inside contour of the ear.

Sid became aware of the woman who was watching with growing interest and some measure of disgust. He made eye contact with her and glanced down at his plate repeatedly, encouraging her to watch. At his prompting, she hesitantly returned her gaze to the potato bunny once more.

Sid took hold of either side of his plate and bobbed it up and down on the table cloth, giving it a half-turn back and forth each time, animating his bunny, simulating it running merrily along. He hummed a silly tune, like something from a pre-schooler cartoon show, and it seemed an appropriate fit.

The woman couldn't help but smile, half-amused, even as she remained appalled by the childish table manners. Once he had her undivided attention, Sid stopped, releasing the plate and grabbing his steak knife. He vigorously sawed through the potato bunny's throat, making a soft, high-pitched scream on its behalf. The woman's eyes widened in horror as Sid continued sawing and screaming until he hit the gravy core. Thick dark fluid spilled out of the bunny's neck and Sid changed his sound effect to a long, drawn-out hacking gurgle.

Conversation at the table ground to a halt as everyone turned to see what the disturbance was. Sid's bunny death-rattle dragged on, growing fainter, until it ended with a final hack and sputter as he completely separated the head from the body.

Sid picked up a fork, scooped a large mound of gravy-soaked mashed potatoes, and shoveled it sloppily into his mouth.

"Mmm, bunny flesh," he commented.

Louise returned to the dining room at that moment and observed Sid eating when her attention was drawn to the sole silent table.

"Mr. Volke," she said, "I see you've found something to suit your dietary requirements."

"These are the best mashed potatoes I've ever had," he told her, pointing at them with his fork. "So rich. What's your secret?"

"If I'm not mistaken, you skin potatoes, boil them and mash them. With butter and perhaps a bit of salt?"

Catering had taken care of the potatoes, and everything else on the menu, but Louise still remembered her way around kitchen basics.

"Butter!" exclaimed Sid. "That's the secret. Who'd have thought? I gotta try that next time. I was thinking about planting potatoes in the spring."

It was an ambitious agricultural plan. Sid wondered if he'd be able to find another bathtub by planting season. Something he could pull out of the trash and drag up to his apartment. He'd fill it with dirt and use it for a new crop. Potatoes were an option, though beans would probably be easier.

"Well, do eat up," encouraged Louise. "For a donation of ten thousand dollars, you've certainly paid for the privilege."

Sid nearly choked on his next mouthful of mash.

Benton arrived in the dining room and gave his wife an affectionate peck on the cheek. He then placed a hand on Sid's shoulder and mentioned, "I don't think we've collected your contribution yet. Would you mind terribly, before dessert is served?"

Sid wiped the gravy off his chin with a napkin as he got up.

"I'll just get my cheque book," he said. "I think it's in my other tuxedo."

►►▌

Sid took a sharp left turn at the stairs and took the steps three at a time. Once he arrived at the second-floor hallway, he quickly passed from room to room, ducking his head in each until he found the one Alexandra was in.

"We have to get the hell out of here," he told her, shutting the door behind him. "Apparently I just ate ten grand worth of mashed potatoes."

The room was nearly dark. Alexandra had risked a bit of light, switching on a desk lamp as she made her sweep.

"There's nothing here!" she hissed in frustration. "No DVD, VCR. No computer, no laptop, not even a phone that isn't a land line. Apparently they're so old, they think television is a passing fad."

The room appeared to be a study. Lined with books and files, there was nothing remotely high-tech enough to house the sexual indiscretions of Helen St. Simone.

"There has to be something," Sid insisted. "What about this?"

A covered keyboard sat on the desk. Sid pulled the fitted sheet off it, revealing an electric typewriter from decades past.

"Right," said Alexandra, who had looked there first. "You wipe the hard drive, I'll yank the ethernet cable."

"Maybe there's a safe," Sid suggested.

They looked around again, but there was nothing. No safe, no locked drawers or boxes. There was only one electrical outlet in the entire room, and the only things plugged into it were the desk lamp and the typewriter.

"If the tape is here, there's nothing to view it with, let alone transfer it," Alexandra concluded.

"How many rooms did you check?"

Sid was still considering if there might be a secret server room tucked away in the basement, next to the wine cellar, when the overhead lights snapped on. Benton Manning stood in the doorway with Franklin right behind him. Louise, out in the hall, looked over their shoulders with concern.

"If you're after my choicest valuables," said Benton, "I have a superb collection of 18th-century military insignia in the library."

"You know what we're looking for," said Alexandra, defiantly refusing to be embarrassed by being caught snooping red-handed.

"There are plenty of cheques made out to my foundation," Benton told her, "but very little cash on hand, I assure you."

"Don't play the innocent benefactor," Alexandra sneered. "It might fool those high-society museum pieces you're trying to entertain downstairs, but not us."

"We know you're running the biggest adult-performer agency on the east coast," said Sid, "and you're using your boy here as a front man so your good name doesn't get tainted by the sex industry."

Franklin's eyes narrowed when he was mentioned, but Benton spoke for him.

"Franklin is my driver. Has been for years. I trust him implicitly to pick up my dry cleaning. Anything beyond travelling from point A to point B I take care of myself."

Louise was taken aback by the accusation.

"Benton? A pornographer? Please!"

She very nearly laughed at the notion.

"Look," Sid assured her, "I know it's hard to believe..."

But Louise would have none of it.

"If anyone here is a pornographer, it's me," she said.

The kindly old lady's admission caught Sid and Alexandra off guard.

"I'm sure it's hard to imagine now," she continued, "but I was in the business back when Montreal was Sin City North. It wasn't all pole dances and web cameras in those days. It was burlesque and stag films. There was still a mystique to it. Smut was dirty, shameful, the way it's meant to be. Benton lifted me out of all that. It was a terrible scandal at the time, but he stood by me. If you want to drag all that out again, do your worst, but I must ask you to leave our home immediately, Mr. Volke. And you, young Miss."

Louise turned and descended the stairs, returning to her guests, but she couldn't mask her sadness.

With his wife departed, Benton Manning took on a harsher tone. Any pretense of geniality in light of this personal intrusion vanished in an instant.

"You've made a spectacle of yourselves and you've upset my wife," he said. "Franklin, if they're not here to behave themselves and make a charitable donation, then they're leaving. Show them out at once."

Franklin stepped forward without a word, but his cold unblinking stare spoke more menace than any verbalized threat. Sid took a step back and put up his fists, ready to defend himself and Alexandra.

"You want to get rough?" he said. "There's a policeman downstairs right now."

Benton patted the breast pocket of his suit at the reminder.

"I know," he said. "I have his department's cheque right here."

Benton left Franklin to do his thing as he returned to his wife's side.

By the time Sid was physically ejected from the house, his coiffed hair was a mess and his tuxedo wrinkled and torn. He hadn't put up more than token resistance, but Franklin had twisted his arm behind his back and made sure that the short journey to the exit was a rough ride. The final shove out the door nearly sent Sid rolling down the path, but flailing arms and a lucky stumble kept him on his feet.

"Hey!" he shouted back at the house. "I didn't come here alone!"

Alexandra was flung from the door next. Barefoot, she landed on her ass in the mud. Her shoes were thrown from the house moments later, landing in a puddle next to her, splashing both of them.

"Okay," said Sid with a wave, "thank you."

Sid helped Alexandra to her feet.

"I've been kicked out of better Golden Globe parties than this!" she spat. "Assholes!"

She struggled to get her wet shoes back on before leaving the property.

Benton stood in the doorway, making sure the couple departed without further incident. Most of the party had gathered behind him to watch the commotion. Langelier squeezed his way through the crowd.

"Is there a problem, Monsieur Manning?" he asked his host.

"Nothing I can't take care of myself," Benton assured him.

Sid and Alexandra walked through the dark, moneyed streets of Westmount, looking worse for wear. They were overdressed for an evening stroll, but the torn seams of Sid's rental tux and Alexandra's twisted and dishevelled evening gown took them down a few notches. Sid pulled off his clip-on bow tie and stuffed it deep in a pocket.

"It's chilly," said Alexandra.

"It's winter," replied Sid.

Sid took his hands out of his muddy pockets, shrugged off his black jacket, and draped it over Alexandra's shoulders.

"I'm starting to think it's all hype. When does the snow get here?"

"Whenever it damn well pleases," said Sid, speaking from a decade of experience. "We should call a cab."

Alexandra pulled the remains of her cell phone from her purse. Crushed in the melee, it was now a collection of cracked plastic and broken glass. She tossed it into a trash can at the edge of the park they were passing.

"I would if I could."

Sid sat down on a park bench and patted the space next to him, encouraging Alexandra to join him. She did.

"You know, I was happy for you when I heard you'd settled down, got married, bought a house," she said.

"So was I," agreed Sid.

"What the hell happened?"

"It was my last gig as a paparazzo," Sid told her. "I got assigned to Chase Mosaic. Remember her?"

Alexandra searched her mental Rolodex.

"Pop-star flash-in-the-pan."

Sid nodded.

"There are plenty of one-hit wonders, she was more of a three-hit wonder. It looked like she might get fifteen minutes plus, and I was following her to every club, every premiere, every concert. Just snapping pictures. You see somebody every day, you get friendly. You get friendly, you end up in some of the shots."

"You get too friendly, you get screwed," added Alexandra.

"My wife saw a picture of us together in the tabloids and figured I must be banging her."

"Jealous," noted Alexandra, knowing all too well how these things played out.

"And right," said Sid.

"She took everything?"

"I got the cat."

"You got screwed."

"Fair trade," said Sid. "I love that cat."

Sid took a pause on memory lane.

"After that I ran."

"To here?" asked Alexandra. "You don't even speak the language."

"I speak English and I speak street," said Sid. "Which means I understand about two-thirds of what gets said. Two-thirds is close enough. Besides, there's no celebrity bullshit to deal with."

"There are always celebrities," said Alexandra. "Everywhere you go now, somebody's famous for something."

"Yeah, but once anybody gets big here, they leave. Celine went to Vegas, Shatner's been in Hollywood forever. The ones who stay are small potatoes and I can deal with them. It's the superstars I can't stomach. The Helen St. Simones of the world."

"It's all head shots and press releases and spin doctoring," said Alexandra of her trade. "She's a regular person just like the rest of us. The only difference is she believes her own press."

"Ah," said Sid. "You mean the celebrity bullshit *you* create."

"Guilty as charged."

Alexandra still looked cold. Sid put his arm around her.

"Keep me warm," he said.

Blow Out

December 29th

THE SUN WAS up but Sid and Alexandra weren't. They had fallen asleep on the park bench, leaning into each other in an awkward position that would make for sore muscles in the coming days. Their mouths hung open, alternately snoring or drooling, sometimes both at once. A curt bleat of a siren disturbed the tableau, waking them both with a start.

They rubbed their eyes and found themselves staring at a couple of officers in a Westmount patrol car that had pulled up to the curb across from them.

"Hey!" said the one on the passenger side through his open window, "No loitering here. Move along."

Sid lifted his hand sleepily in a motion that waved at them and shooed them away at once. Westmount had its very own public-safety department. They weren't cops, but they knew how to hassle people just like the real thing.

Sid rose to his feet with a groan and helped Alexandra up.

"Right," he said, "I forgot. This neighbourhood is too rich to let anybody sleep on a park bench."

"I guess you're allowed to patronize the homeless here, you just can't be one," said Alexandra.

Sid and Alexandra completed their walk of shame an hour later—an early morning return in evening-only wear. The few people about made sure to spare them long, embarrassing stares as they turned up the final street to Sid's flat in their soiled and torn party clothes.

Up the winding stairs, Sid let them into his apartment. He took one look at the disarray of the place and declared, "Oh my God, I've been ransacked!"

To Alexandra, it looked exactly the same as it always did.

"How can you tell?" she asked.

Sid flicked on a light. Instantly, a huge, looming, fang-faced shadow fell across them. He and Alexandra both recoiled in terror until they looked up and saw Hoagy looking down at them from inside a large bowl-shaped light fixture on the ceiling. The light behind him cast a large shadow as he observed them from over the glass lip.

"Hoagy?" said Sid. "What are you doing up there?"

There was no explanation beyond a single, pathetic meow.

"Some guard cat you are," Sid told him.

Alexandra stepped over the destruction as Sid wandered through his home, taking inventory of new damage only he could perceive.

"Well, I think we touched a nerve last night," he announced.

"I kinda figured that one out the moment we got tossed out on our ear," said Alexandra.

"Yeah, but what were they looking for here?"

"They must think we have the tape."

"Which means they don't have it either," concluded Sid. "Breakfast?"

Sid ducked into the bathroom long enough to pluck one of his onions from the miniature garden in the sink.

"I'll skip, thanks," said Alexandra. "I like something to go with my onions. Like an actual meal."

Sid peeled the onion, letting the skin and dirt cascade to the floor. He bit into it like a ripe apple. Alexandra turned away, unable to stomach Sid's eating habits so early in the morning after a poor night's sleep in the cold.

She looked in the bedroom for the remaining cat.

"Sabrina? You okay, honey? Come out come out wherever you are."

A rustling noise in the dark room drew her further inside. Everything had been tossed around or tipped over. Only the laundry hamper remained upright.

"They didn't touch the hamper," she informed Sid.

"Ha!" he responded. "I told you. That thing's my personal bank vault."

"What do you keep in there? Your life savings?"

"Life savings? Please!" Sid laughed. "That sort of thing costs money. I told you, I keep my valuables in there."

"I shudder to think what you call valuables."

There was more noise from the shadowy corners of the room.

"Sabrina?" Alexandra asked again.

"You find her?"

Adjusting to the dark, Alexandra spotted a pair of eyes staring back at her.

"No," she said, "it's your goddamn raccoon again."

"Pork Chop?" said Sid, as he watched the raccoon wander out from behind the couch, far from where Alexandra was looking.

The eyes in the dark suddenly leapt forward. Alexandra saw that they belonged to a man in a ski mask just before he tackled her to the floor and put his hands around her throat.

Sid heard the struggle in the next room and shouted, "Alex!"

Before he could go to assist Alexandra, a second masked man emerged from the pile of bedding jumbled on the floor from the previous night's sleepover. He rushed Sid and body checked him into a wall, denting the plaster. Sid grabbed hold of his assailant by the back of his knees and tipped them both over, resulting in a wrestling match that rolled across the living-room refuse.

The twin struggles in two different rooms continued until Alexandra, reaching for something—anything—tipped the laundry hamper over onto the masked man who was trying to pin her. There was a delayed reaction as the stench of Sid's dirty clothes seeped through his mask, but when he got a nose full, the man loosened his grip long enough to shrug off the sweaty garments. Alexandra found herself with enough space to wiggle out from under her attacker and make a break for the kitchen. She didn't get far. Just as she crossed the threshold, her masked man dove and grabbed her by the ankles. Alexandra toppled forward and hit the linoleum hard.

Fighting through the jolt of pain and the darkness that was creeping in from her peripheral vision, Alexandra rolled onto her back and looked for a new weapon. Staring up from the floor, she could see all the cupboards had been opened in the search, all the drawers pulled out. Pots and pans littered the area, temptingly close. She tried to crawl for one, but the man held her ankles tight, keeping her from making any progress farther than a few inches.

Alexandra strained to perform a single sit-up from her awkward position, and brought herself close enough to the man's head to grab a handful of his ski mask and tear it off, exposing Carlos. Instinctively, Carlos tried to hide his identity by covering his face with his hands, letting go of Alexandra in the process. It gave her enough slack to reach her choice of frying pan.

Carlos spread his fingers apart on his face so he could see. It looked like he was playing a game of peek-a-boo with a child. He managed a brief glimpse of the flat underside of the pan coming down on his head. After that, there was only black nothing.

In the next room, the other intruder had Sid in a bear hug. With his forearms crushed up against his attacker's chest, Sid could only paw at the man's face, poking him in the eyes, pulling at his lips, and sticking various fingers up his nose. Eventually he worked two fingers into the eye sockets of the mask and pulled it off to reveal Randy Dix underneath.

Sid swung a leg up over Randy's hip and planted it against a nearby wall. Kicking off, he managed to send both himself and Randy crashing back to the floor. Randy was a bigger man than Sid, with far more muscle on him. He easily overpowered Sid once he was on top, pinning him in place, crushing the wind out of him. With their faces only inches apart, Sid used the only weapon left to him, exhaling straight up into Randy's face.

Randy's nose flared and his eyes began to water under the assault of Sid's raw-onion morning breath.

"Arg!" he exlaimed, "Son of a bitch maced me!"

With Randy's grip loosening, Sid rolled the big man off and struggled to his feet. Randy also got up, but flailed blindly as he wiped tears from his eyes. It was too tempting a target. Sid drew his foot back, winding up, and then delivered a savage kick straight into Randy's testicles.

"Not the money maker..." Randy groaned, cupping his balls before keeling over into a fetal position.

Carlos was still out cold in the kitchen. He showed no signs of life as Sid and Alexandra finished tying Randy to a chair for safekeeping. Although Randy had managed to remain conscious, his aching groin had kept him from putting up much of a fight while he was being secured in place.

"Don't bother telling us who sent you," said Sid, as he pulled the final knot tight. "I know it was your pimp, Franklin. He's already looking at a murder one. You two idiots have only racked up a B and E and a couple counts of assault. Be good and maybe it won't even come to that."

"Just let me go," winced Randy. "Forget I was ever here."

"So what happened?" asked Sid, looking around at the even more dismal state of his apartment. "You were searching the place and you ran out of time?"

"Yeah, not enough time," agreed Randy impatiently. "Let me outta here, okay?"

Randy tried to pull his wrist free of the clothesline that fixed it to one arm of the chair and found it to be tighter than he anticipated. Sid ignored the fruitless struggle and continued his line of questioning.

"It's Manning who's really in charge, right? Pulling Franklin's strings. Sponging off every porn shoot in town."

Randy was sweating, frightened.

"Sure, yeah, I guess," he said, though he was too distracted to focus on Sid's interrogation.

Alexandra snapped her fingers in front of Randy's face a few times to get his attention.

"Hey!" she said firmly, trying to get Randy to focus. "Benton Manning! Right?"

But Randy's mind remained elsewhere.

"What?" he said, "Who?"

"Useless!" declared Alexandra, throwing her arms up in frustration.

"Look, you gotta let me go!" Randy pleaded. "Let me out or I'll fuck your shit up!" he added, enraged.

Randy's desperation was palpable, his emotions all over the place. Sid was unimpressed.

"My shit's been fucked up so long, I wouldn't even notice," he told Randy.

"I swear, I'll kill you!" Randy shouted back.

He strained against his ropes and hopped in place, but the chair barely budged more than an inch.

"Oooo, big bad biker man," Alexandra taunted, unconvinced.

Sid stopped cold the moment he heard Alexandra's comment.

"Wait, what was that?"

"Nothing," Alexandra assured Sid. "He was trying to impress me yesterday, telling me he used to be in a gang."

"Don't try to tell me about gangs, tough guy," she said to Randy. "I'm from the City of Angels."

Sid returned his attention to Randy. He didn't share Alexandra's dismissive attitude. Instead, he became sharply focused and deadly serious.

"You're in a biker gang?" he asked.

Randy tried to downplay his answer.

"I've done the occasional contract."

Sid grabbed the arms of the chair that bound Randy in place and brought his face very close to his prisoner's.

"Is this a hit?" he asked softly, but very distinctly.

Randy said nothing, but Sid studied his eyes closely and found an answer in them he didn't like. He turned to Alexandra, suddenly very agitated.

"Get out!" Sid commanded. "Get out now! Pack up the cats and run!"

Alexandra almost laughed at Sid's dramatic intensity.

"What's the matter? These two assholes aren't going to hurt anyone. They don't even have guns."

Sid ignored her and turned back to Randy, roaring, "Where is it?"

"Just let me go, man!" was the only response he got from Randy, who had dropped the threats and returned to a pleading strategy to gain his freedom.

Sid wasn't listening anymore. He was tearing the place apart, searching through the mess for something specific. It would likely take hours to find any one item in all that junk, but Sid seemed determined to discover it in the next couple of minutes.

Alexandra didn't understand Sid's sense of urgency, but followed his instructions just the same. Setting a small step ladder back on its feet, she climbed up the few steps, positioning herself under the hallway light fixture, and tried to coax Hoagy down.

"It's okay, honey," she assured the cat, "the bad men can't hurt you now."

At this point, Hoagy seemed more concerned with his master. Sid was digging furiously through the refuse, leaping from one random pile to the next.

Hooking her thumbs under Hoagy's front legs, Alexandra was able to draw him forward and over the glass rim of the light. Once the cat was in her arms, she informed Sid, "You're just making a bigger mess, you know."

"Where the hell did you put it, you dumb prick!" Sid yelled at Randy.

Alexandra stepped down off the ladder, cradling Sid's cat.

"What are you looking for?" she asked, amused by the theatrics. "The keys to his Harley?"

Sid didn't slow his search any, but explained on the fly, "The biker gangs here, they're not really motorcycle enthusiasts as such. They're more like a drug cartel who settle their differences by blowing each other up. Cars and bars mostly, but they'll plant explosives anywhere that suits them."

Sid's frantic hunt didn't seem quite so silly anymore.

"You're saying there's a bomb in here?"

"Ask the demolition expect!" said Sid, pointing a finger sharply at Randy.

"It wasn't my idea, I swear!" sputtered Randy in his defence. "Franklin insisted. He said it was orders from the top. What could I do? They run it all now! I gotta eat!"

Alexandra backed towards the door with Hoagy. Her eyes darted around the apartment.

"Sid!" she said fearfully. "I don't know where Sabrina is."

Sid waved a hand at her, insisting, "I'll get her! Go!"

Alexandra paused briefly, considering her options, wondering what else she could save from imminent destruction. Tucking Hoagy under one arm, she grabbed the edge of Sushi's bowl and took the fish with her as well as she departed.

Sid switched his search from somewhere a biker might stash a bomb to places where a cat might try to hide during a home invasion. The kitchen offered the best options.

As soon as he left the room, Randy started hopping up and down, violently trying to free himself.

"Get me the fuck out of this chair!" he screamed, more a prayer than a plea to Sid, who was indifferent to the danger Randy had put himself in.

Stepping over Carlos, Sid looked in the cabinets under the counter.

"Here puss-puss! Here girl!"

The cupboards over the sink proved more fruitful. Sabrina was in the third one Sid checked, poking through a box of breakfast cereal, helping herself to a snack.

"There you are!" exclaimed Sid, relieved.

He shoved the box out of the way so he could grab the cat, but froze in mid-reach. The bomb he'd so desperately wanted to find was there, right behind the box—two sticks of dynamite wired to a timer. There were only seconds left on the digital display.

Meanwhile, Randy's frantic hopping paid off. The wooden chair broke under him on the last jump, loosening the ropes and setting him free. He ran for a window overlooking the back of the building and struggled to unlatch it.

Sid grabbed the bomb and placed it on the counter. He fiddled with the wires briefly, considering whether he should pull one of them, none of them, or all of them. Thinking better of any of those options, he instead tossed the explosives into his near-empty fridge and slammed the door shut.

Grabbing Sabrina by the scruff of the neck, Sid ran out of the kitchen. There was no more time left to make it out of the building safely so he went for the most heavily reinforced room available. Kicking open the door to the bathroom, Sid dove into the tub, flattening his tomato crop and burying his face in the dirt.

Carlos, groggy and in pain, slowly sat up in time to see his partner throw himself out the back window.

"Hey Randy," he said, "where you going?"

But Randy was already free-falling towards a hard landing on the concrete patio below.

Carlos put a hand on his aching skull and declared, "Ow, my fuckin' h..."

A tremendous bang blew out all the windows on Sid's floor at once. Alexandra, watching from the street, was knocked off her feet. Every car alarm on the block went off from the concussion.

Alexandra hugged Hoagy close to keep the terrified feline from bolting. She looked up and saw licks of flame around the windows and door of Sid's apartment. Small bits of debris rained down from the blast, covering the road. They were punctuated by one giant piece. Just as she was trying to rise to her feet to get a better look at the damage, the entire refrigerator, scorched and with the door blown clean off, came crashing down on the roof of the car right behind her. Alexandra was sprayed by cubes of safety glass from the car windows as the top of the vehicle was pancaked into the bucket seats.

"Sid!" she shrieked over the drone of honking horns and alarms.

There were no signs of life in the building for several long moments before Sid came stumbling out of his front door. He had taken a moment to pull on his poor excuse for a winter coat, but it had been cut to ribbons by the blast. Half sliding, half tumbling down his twisting iron staircase, he arrived at ground level.

Sid was a gruesome mess as he staggered out to meet Alexandra. The sight of him turned her stomach. Red chunks of mashed pulp dripped off of him from all over, and his face was covered in gore.

"Oh my God, Sid!" she exclaimed. If he was half as wounded as he looked, it was amazing he was even standing.

"I'm okay," Sid assured her. "It's not me. It's my tomatoes."

Alexandra instantly switched to her next point of dire concern.

"Where's Sabrina?"

"Don't worry," said Sid. "I got her."

But Sid wasn't carrying any cat.

"Where?" asked Alexandra.

Sid pulled back one side of his long coat, revealing Sabrina. She was clinging to his leg, frozen in fear, her claws embedded in Sid's thigh. Sid winced in pain as Alexandra extracted Sabrina's claws from his leg, one digit at a time.

With Sabrina and Hoagy both tucked under Alexandra's arms, Sid looked down and saw Sushi's fish

bowl overturned on the pavement. His fish was flop-
ping around in a puddle on the street.

Grabbing the bowl, Sid limped away to the opposite row of houses. One of his neighbours had been
out washing his car with a garden hose in the unsea-
sonably mild weather when the bomb went off. He
was still staring at the scene dumbfounded. Sid took
the hose from him, filled the fish bowl with it, and
returned to the middle of the road. He gingerly
picked up his gasping goldfish and dropped it into the
water, where it eagerly resumed swimming.

"Let's move," said Sid. "Far away and fast."

Bundling up the pets, Sid and Alexandra hurried
away down the street as sirens approached. Pork
Chop was the last to vacate the premises. No one
who came outside to see what had happened paid the
urban raccoon any mind as he trotted to the next
block over in search of a new place to call home.

▶▶▌

Away from the growing crowd of curious onlookers,
Randy picked himself up off the postage stamp of a
backyard that rested behind Sid's building. The concrete had made for a rough landing, but had failed to
break any bones. Randy's main concern was that he
wouldn't grow any unsightly bruises on parts of his
anatomy that featured prominently in his films.

Slowly, achingly, he got back on his feet and
shambled through the sheets of hanging laundry until

he found the wooden fence at the back of the yard. Only once he was there did he notice the blasted refrigerator door sticking out of the wall of a garage on the next lot. More prominent was the body of Carlos, hanging over the broken boards of the fence where the explosion had propelled him.

Randy turned away from his fallen partner, un-latched the gate, and let himself out into the lane that ran behind the rows of houses. He looked up one end and down the other for the car that was supposed to be waiting. There was no sign of it. It was possible it had circled the block once or twice so as not to draw suspicion while it waited for the rendezvous, but Randy was worried. He knew he was behind schedule. They were all supposed to be long gone before the bomb went off. Now there would be fire trucks, ambulances and police cars to avoid. Plus Carlos was dead. His body would be identified, questions would be asked. The entire search, bombing and murder plot had been a colossal failure, and Randy longed for the good old days of the biker wars when these sorts of things always seemed to come off without a hitch. He was desperate to get away, but wouldn't blame his ride one bit if it had ditched him.

Just when he was about to hop the opposite fence and make his way to the next parallel street, the car appeared at the mouth of the lane. Dark and with tinted windows, he couldn't quite make out the driver behind the wheel, but knew it had to be Franklin. His ride was so distinct, Randy knew his representation wouldn't want it to be spotted and remembered at the scene of a crime. The fact that he had swung by one final time to search for his missing people before the whole area got roped off by cop cars and crime-scene tape reassured Randy that signing with him might have been the smart move after all. Franklin had his back.

The car turned into the lane and sped up. Randy tried to wave it down, but the vehicle passed right by him like he wasn't even there.

"Hey wait!" shouted Randy, amazed Franklin failed to recognize him. "It's me! Come back!"

The car came to an abrupt halt at the far end of the alley and began to back up. Relieved, Randy jogged towards it despite the complaints of his sore limbs. The car picked up speed as it continued to reverse. Too late, Randy realized he wasn't being picked up, he was being targeted. He tried to leap out of the way, but his battered joints were slow to respond. The rear bumper cut him off at the knees and one of the back tires rolled right over his torso.

The car idled for a moment, as if surveying the damage it had done to itself. The back right corner was heavily dented by the impact. Randy's blood dripped from the wheel well. The injury was unsightly, but easily corrected with a car wash and a trip to a body shop.

There was a second figure in the car. This one rode in the back seat. Behind the tinted glass, a hand was raised, and a slight wave bade the driver to advance.

Shifting gears, the rear tire rolled over Randy's body a second time as the car drove back down the lane and turned onto the cross street at the end.

Sid and Alexandra sat side-by-side at the back of a city bus in their destroyed evening wear, holding one cat each, and supporting a sloshing fish bowl on the seat between them. The thin trail of smoke behind them, rising above the skyline from Sid's apartment, grew smaller and more distant with each stop.

As new passengers were collected, they joined the others who were already staring at the pair and their menagerie.

Alexandra kept her eyes fixed straight ahead. When she spoke at last, she sounded numb.

"I can't believe I saved the goddamn goldfish and not my gold card."

"Thanks for that," said Sid. "Sushi thanks you, too."

"Where are we going to run with no money?"

"As far as bus fare takes us."

It took one bus, a metro transfer, and a second express bus to see them to a safe harbour. Ultimately, once their meagre options were considered and dismissed as too impractical, too expensive, or too unsafe, Alexandra suggested the one place familiar to her that might respond to pleas for sympathy and questionable credit.

"Hi, remember me?" Alexandra began. "You know, the last time I was here, with the traumatic experience and all that? Right. Well, I've had a few more traumas since then and..."

She trailed off, not sure if she was getting through to the manager of the airport motel she'd stayed at so very briefly. Sid hung back with the collection of pets while Alexandra stated her case.

"Look," Alexandra continued, "the thing is, I have no money, I have no cards, but you know me and you saw that I did have plenty of cash and credit just a few days ago. And I really need a place to stay while I call Visa and Master Card and American Express and explain to them how all their plastic exploded at the same time, and how I really need new cards issued right away so I don't end up sleeping in the gutter."

A slow dawning of recognition crossed the manager's face as Alexandra ran through her petition for mercy. There was a pathetic charm to it that made an impression. When, at last, she came to her halting conclusion, the manager sighed and succumbed to pity.

►►|

Alexandra had been comped a room before, but she'd never had to beg to be comped. And, in past comping instances, the understanding was that the

room was free—not free until one or more credit
cards showed up by emergency courier for an enormous service charge. Humiliating or not, a second-
level room had been secured. It had a bed and, more
importantly, a shower that allowed Sid and Alexandra
to clean up after a day of vicious manhandling and
explosions. The moment they were both freshly
washed, they'd fallen asleep together, spooning on
the double bed, too exhausted to care about the inad-
vertent cuddle they'd gravitated to in their stupor.
They both slept in their underwear. Sid had a pair of
boxers on, leaving his leg, covered with a dozen
Band-aids to patch Sabrina's claw marks, above the
sheets to keep the layers of linen from pressing down
on his many fresh wounds. The cats slept at their feet,
curled into balls. Even the fish dozed in its bowl on
the end table next to the phone.

After several hours of desperately needed rest,
Alexandra began to wake from her deep nap. She
soon realized Sid's hand was cupped over one breast.
It was a non-sexual gesture. Sid was dead to the world.

"Sid?" Alexandra said.

"Mmm?" was the only answer she got.

"Boob."

Sid moved his hand without waking.

Sid and Alexandra came down to reception to speak
with the manager once they were both up and had

made themselves more presentable. Their clothes were still a shredded mess, but Alexandra had requested and received a needle and thread from housekeeping. The spool of thread had been a bright green that didn't match anything, but she achieved enough of a repair with it to keep their outfits together until something better could be found. Alexandra kept Sid's tuxedo jacket. Sid was satisfied with his old coat over the black pants and white shirt. He threw away the bow tie as useless, even though it was the only part of the ensemble the rental place might have accepted back. Alexandra was resigned to eating the expense of a replacement just as soon as she had credit to her name again.

When they returned the borrowed sewing kit to the front desk, Sid busied himself inspecting the primitive motel security-camera system.

"The police took the tape," the manager explained to Alexandra. "The one with their suspect coming and going. They said they might be able to enhance it or something."

"How often do you swap these tapes?" Sid asked.

"Whenever they run out," answered the manager. "I always set them to record on the slow speed, so we get about six hours out of them."

"How soon before the murder did you swap tapes?"

"Probably about an hour."

"You still have the tape that was running right before the one the cops took?"

The manager picked through his pile of used tapes that were queued to be reused in the coming shifts.

"What are you thinking?" said Alexandra.

"Manning and his goon, Franklin," said Sid. "They can't have the home movie we're after. Whoever does came and went before the murder happened."

The manager ejected the current recording tape and popped another one into the surveillance system. He pressed play and fast-forwarded through a lot of mundane parking-lot footage until Sid stopped him. A lone figure could be seen approaching the motel, but headed for the exterior stairs rather than the front office.

"There!" said Sid, tapping the screen with a finger. "That's who we're looking for. The buyer. The killer came by after him and erased any evidence of the deal, but this is who actually made the deal."

"You don't know that," said Alexandra. "He could be anyone."

The manager rewound and ran through the segment again in slow motion.

"What's he carrying?" Sid asked, his nose only inches away from the monitor.

"I can't tell," said Alexandra, squinting. "The resolution's crap."

The manager hit the pause button.

"It's too small to be a suitcase," concluded Sid after a few moments of scrutiny.

"A laptop computer?" suggested Alexandra.

"No," said Sid at last. "It's a VCR to hook up so he can watch the merchandise in the room and assess how much it's worth. We know he cut a cheque then and there. That's because he knew what he had was golden."

The manager fast-forwarded again until the same figure returned, retracing his route, this time leaving the motel.

"And here he is walking away with the goods," said Sid. "Manning doesn't have the tape. This guy does."

"But who is he?" wondered Alexandra.

"Recognize the girth?" Sid asked her.

Alexandra ran through her mental list of everybody she'd met in Montreal since setting down. She ignored the faces and tried to remember the body types.

"Marty Guerin?" she asked, and saw that's who Sid was thinking of as well. "Maybe, but we can't be sure."

"We're not the police," Sid reminded her. "We don't have to be sure enough to get a search warrant, we just need to be sure enough to act on a hunch."

A call rang on the front-desk phone. The manager picked up and had a brief exchange with one of the occupied rooms before setting the receiver down again with the assurance, "I'll take care of it at once."

"That was a complaint," he told his freeloading guests. "There is a horrible noise coming from your room."

"They've found us!" Alexandra declared.

Sid dashed off to confront to the intruders. Alexandra reluctantly followed. Up on the second-floor walkway, Sid paused outside their motel room. The racket coming from inside was hideous. It sounded like there was another murder in progress. Cautiously, Sid fit the key into the lock and turned it.

Sid and Alexandra burst into the room, ready for a fight. What they found was Hoagy mounting Sabrina on the bed. Both cats were yowling at the top of their lungs as they mated.

"Oh my God," exclaimed Alexandra, "what is your mangy animal doing to my precious baby?"

"You really need me to explain it to you?" said Sid.

Shelter

December 30th

THE WINTER SUN was down early, but Sid and Alexandra waited until it was well past midnight to get their journey back downtown underway. They walked to a nearby terminal off the highway and took a night-bus express to another terminal close to their final destination. A good hike brought them down to the canal, which they followed until the industrial headquarters of Poontang Posse, and a dozen more discreetly named and legitimate start-ups, loomed.

The front door was locked and never an option. Instead, Sid led Alexandra around back to search for a suitable fire escape that hugged the outer wall of the suite they wanted. Boosting Alexandra up on his shoulders, she was able to grab the edge of the weighted stairs and swing them down to the parking-lot tarmac. Sid scaled the interconnecting ladders until he arrived at the correct level and could judge his best point of entry.

Not all of the fixtures and fittings had been up-dated during the refurbishment of the old factory. On his previous visit, Sid had noticed that some of the original windows had been retained. It didn't take long patrolling along the fire-escape scaffolding to find one of them, and with the help of a coat hanger from the motel, he was able to force a wire loop through a narrow crack in the window frame and hook the old-fashioned latch on the inside. With a sharp tug, he pulled the latch to the left and pushed the window open from the outside.

Despite all his efforts at stealth, Sid managed to come spilling into the room with a deafening clatter once he swung his leg inside and failed to find his footing. He stumbled around in the dark, tripping over everything in his way, until he fell with another crash. It was Alexandra, coming in behind him, who more successfully navigated the pitfalls and found the light switch first.

The overheads snapped on and Sid found himself face-to-face with a long and intimidating strap-on dildo. The rig hung from a costume rack along with a broad selection of other fetishistic outfits. At least he'd broken into the right place—Alexandra had been worried they'd wind up in a different type of sweat shop and would be all night breaking into vari-ous suites until they found the correct one.

"I nearly put my eye out on that thing," said Sid, as he edged away from the mighty rubber phallus.

"I don't think that's where it's meant to go," commented Alexandra.

Sid clambered to his feet and looked around. They found themselves in the Poontage Posse prop room. Sex toys of all shapes, sizes and battery requirements filled the shelves.

"See any souvenirs you'd care to take home to remind you of your vacation in *la belle province*?" asked Sid.

"The only plastic toy that ever got me off was my gold card," Alexandra lamented.

Sid had the penlight that he always kept in his coat pocket—one of his only possessions to survive the apartment blast. He switched it on and led them out of the prop room and into the dark studio beyond.

The editing bay was in the next room over. Sid made his way down the row of computers, shining light on each one in turn. Every single DVD ROM tray had been ejected and discs littered the floor.

"Someone's been through here already," said Sid, "looking for digital copies of the tape."

Each of the computer cases were lit up with a single flickering blue light. The distinct sound of a dozen different internal hard drives grinding away could be heard. Sid tapped randomly on a keyboard and one of the monitors switched back on, coming out of sleep mode. A progress bar and some plain technical text told the story of what all the machines in the room were up to.

"The hard drives are all reformatting themselves," Sid told Alexandra. "Everything's been wiped."

"Someone wants to make sure they own the only copy," suggested Alexandra.

Sid's light found a portable piece of equipment that grabbed his interest. It had slots for both VHS and discs.

"Check it out," said Sid. "It's a VCR with a DVD burner and video-capture card. If this is what Marty brought to the motel with him, he could have made a digital master of the tape anytime from the moment he met with your girl."

"But who has the master now?"

Something crunched underfoot with the next step Sid took. He pointed his light at the floor and saw tiny fragments with a metallic surface reflecting back up at him. They were pieces of a DVD, shattered and scattered everywhere. There were other shards as well, many of them large, from more discs that had only been snapped into halves or quarters. Judging from the number of pieces revealed by the narrow beam, there were many dozens of broken discs leading out the second door and into the greater loft area.

Sid and Alexandra followed the trail of splintered silver wedges through the dense forest of porn-movie sets. Sid swung the penlight from one reflecting piece to the next as they went, stopping only when he illuminated one that was accompanied by a scarlet drop of blood. As the number of DVD pieces diminished, the amount of blood on the floor increased. At the end of the path, they discovered the body of Marty Guerin, stretched across the bed of one of his scenes.

The mattress was soaked red from the open wound across his throat. A single large blade of split disc jutted out of the cut. The sharp edge had been used as a weapon of convenience to open his neck like a can of sardines.

Sid slipped his hand under the sheets and used one corner as a buffer between his fingers and the evidence. He gripped the tip of the murder weapon and pulled it out of Marty's neck, setting it down on a pillow. Even through all the blood, he could easily read the truncated marker writing across the back of the DVD. The letters, thickly printed, were "ELE" over "IMO."

"What is it?" asked Alexandra.

"The master Marty made," said Sid. "Or what's left of it. Not to mention what's left of Marty."

"What's an Eleimo?"

"It's not a what. It's a who. Add an 'H' and an 'N' to the first line, and an 'S' and an 'NE' to the second."

Mixed with all the other debris on the floor was a file folder, also stained with blood. It was lying open with a creased legal document on top. Alexandra crouched down to look at it, and Sid offered her more light to see by.

"What have you got?" he asked.

"It's a contract," said Alexandra, and grimly added, "With Helen St. Simone's name on it."

"Is it legit?"

Alexandra examined the familiar signature.

"Looks like it," she said, before noticing a couple of key discrepancies in the pen stroke. "Wait, no. This is Cindy's handwriting. She signed so many things for Helen, it's almost impossible to tell the difference."

"A handwriting expert would be able to say for sure," said Sid. "But that means lawyers and a court case. By the time the sex-tape deal got discredited, Poontang Posse would have made a mint. Even after a settlement, Marty Guerin would have come out ahead of the game."

"You're saying this thing is about to be distributed legitimately?"

"Marty being dead won't stop that now. This master is just a souvenir. It's probably already been to his porn mill and back."

Alexandra stood up again.

"We'll never get the genie back in the bottle now."

"Marty mentioned a distribution centre," Sid began, but quickly trailed off.

"What?" Alexandra prompted.

"The killer has always tried to destroy evidence of Marty's deal. The burnt cheque, the missing video, your dead P.A. So why's all this still lying around for us to find?"

Alexandra looked at the bedding, soggy with blood, glistening wet. A single drop dripped into an expanding puddle on the floor. It was all too fresh.

"Because he's still here," she concluded in a hoarse whisper.

A moment later the entire facade of one of the sets tipped over onto Sid. The stage wall broke over his head and threw him to the floor, covering him and exposing Franklin, who had been hiding behind the structure waiting for his moment to launch an ambush.

Franklin lunged at Alexandra, bounding over the collapsed wall. Sid groaned as Franklin stomped his way across the plywood structure pinning him. Alexandra turned and fled into the studio's collection of backdrops. She and Franklin soon found themselves playing a game of hide-and-seek, from one set to the next, popping in and out of a brothel boudoir, a glory-holed public toilet, a police interrogation room, and a medieval dungeon, before Alexandra was able to lose her pursuer in the jumble of sexual-fantasy scenarios.

Alexandra held her breath as she watched Franklin search for her in the dark studio from her vantage point under the bed in a sleazy motel-room set. He paused only a few feet away, close enough to reach out and touch his polished loafers if she wanted. She was sure he would check under the bed, but then he moved on and was gone from her sight. Just when she started to breathe again, the entire bed rose off the floor and left her completely exposed. Only then did Alexandra realize she had sought shelter under a Murphy bed, and Franklin had flipped the switch to make the entire thing fold itself away into the wall.

Alexandra tried to run again, but Franklin was on her in an instant, grabbing her around the waist. She thrashed furiously, frantic to break free as they knocked over prop furniture left and right before stumbling back into the dungeon set. Manacles hung from chains off the faux-stone walls. Franklin grabbed one and wrapped the links around Alexandra's neck. The set may have been fake, but the chains were real. They dug into her throat, threatening to crush her windpipe as Franklin pulled them tight.

Across the loft, Sid, trying to squirm out from under all the weight on top of him, came to realize it was the Christmas set he'd been clobbered by. Resorting to the one avenue of escape it offered, he wormed his way through the plaster fireplace chimney that was barely wide enough to accommodate him. Free at last, he spotted Alexandra's fight for life against Franklin and looked around for a weapon. The first thing Sid found was a leather gimp costume that had been left draped over a chair following an S&M routine. He decided it would have to do.

Sid came up behind Franklin and pulled the gimp mask down over his head backwards. With the eye holes in the rear, Franklin might as well have been wearing a leather bag. Sid zipped it shut and Franklin released Alexandra while he tried to pull it off. He'd just gotten hold of the zipper when Sid punched him square in his blinded face. Franklin fell back against the dungeon set wall. Alexandra reacted quickly enough to snap one of the manacles around his wrist.

Sid and Alexandra retreated as Franklin tried to go after them. He quickly reached the end of his chain tether and groped for them with his free hand, navigating by the sound of their heavy breathing. With their backs to the neighbouring set, they didn't have much room to manoeuvre, but they managed to stay a few inches out of Franklin's reach as they shuffled along towards the edge.

"Go! Go! Go!" Sid shouted once they were clear.

Together, Sid and Alexandra fled the studio, leaving Franklin chained to the wall and struggling to breathe inside the tight leather mask. Moments later, they were seen running from the building. The lone occupant of a car parked in an empty lot across the street observed their departure through tinted windows. Only once they were gone did the rear door pop open, allowing a figure to emerge.

Back in the studio, Franklin struggled to unzip the reversed mask with his one unbound hand. He finally managed to pull it off his head and fill his lungs with air. Once he finished gasping for breath, he resumed his efforts to free himself, trying to squeeze his hand out of the locked manacle. He was still wrestling with the iron shackle when he heard the elevator arrive in the corridor outside several minutes later.

The door to the studio swung open and light from the hallway fell across Franklin. He hurried to explain himself and his predicament to his employer.

"Guerin is dead, but the other two got away," he reported. "I would have had them, but they locked me in here."

Louise Manning stepped forward and looked at her outwitted operative with contempt.

"It's a prop, you idiot," she said.

Louise reached over and popped open the realistic manacle with a simple twist of a knob. Franklin rubbed his sore wrist, ashamed of himself.

"Clean up in here and we'll deal with them later," his boss instructed him.

"You know where they're going?" Franklin asked.

"I know where they'll be. They only have to figure it out for themselves."

▶▶❙

Sid and Alexandra wandered the back streets of Montreal until the sun was up again. If anyone was out hunting them, they made it as arduous a task as possible, weaving their way through alleys, parks, lanes and cul-de-sacs that weren't quite dead ends for those on foot, willing to hop a fence or two.

After taking the longest route possible, they found themselves in Old Montreal, miles away from where they started, looking out over the harbour water that was bitterly cold, but defiantly refusing to freeze for the winter. The buildings for many blocks all around were charmingly Victorian. Alexandra thought it might even be a nice area to sightsee in, if only the weather weren't miserable, and ruthless pornmongers weren't trying to kill them.

As the morning bled away into the afternoon, it wasn't the chill in the air that finally defeated Alexandra, it was the hunger pangs. The last meal she'd had was a bag of potato chips coated with too much artificial flavour—a ludicrous combination of ketchup and vinegar—purchased from a vending machine at the motel. Before that, it had been a scant few hors d'oeuvres at the crashed Manning party. Fad dieting was all well and good. In L.A., she indulged in it as a matter of routine. But this was approaching starvation. The key difference, she decided, was consent.

"I'm cold," Alexandra complained, building towards her main issue.

Sid put his arm around her as a biting wind came in off the river.

"We can take shelter in a metro station. At least until they kick us out for vagrancy."

"And I'm tired," she added.

"We could hop a turnstile and find a clean bench for you to lie down on," Sid suggested. "Until they kick us out for vagrancy."

"And starving," Alexandra admitted, finally arriving at her most pressing point.

Sid understood the reverse order of priorities all too well. At least he remembered some lessons he'd learned about women from his marriage.

"Let me take you to the hottest spot in town," he offered.

"We have no money."

"I know a place," Sid assured her. "And they won't kick us out for vagrancy."

Alexandra looked at him suspiciously. "I'm not dumpster-diving with you."

"Who said anything about a dumpster?"

"I'm not picking through garbage cans either."

"What kind of animal do you think I am? I'm offering you good food, good company, sparkling conversation. All for a price that can't be beat."

"What's the catch?" Alexandra wanted to know, but not badly enough to refuse Sid's suggestion. Hunger won out over suspicion.

The food wasn't fine dining to be sure, but it was decent, clean, and hot, as promised. The company was, arguably, the salt of the earth. But the conversation didn't exactly sparkle. Most of it was one-sided and muttered, often incomprehensibly, to imaginary friends and memories of loved ones distant or long-dead.

The Mission was one of several of its ilk situated on the outskirts of the oldest end of the city, near the port. It catered to the homeless, the destitute, or those who had fallen on hard times—if only temporarily. Alexandra hoped she was one of the latter, that her misfortune was indeed temporary, and that these hard times would be brief.

Any fear that they were too overdressed to be given shelter and a meal at The Mission was baseless. There were transients and old-school hobos dining in the soup kitchen who looked spiffier than Sid and Alexandra did in their tattered and filthy evening wear. Alexandra realized, to her dismay, that she blended right in with the queue at the cafeteria counter, as she waited for a bowl of fortifying vegetable soup and a bun.

They chose a spot at one of the plain white tables and leaned over their bounty like dogs protecting a bone from others in the pack. There was no need to worry. The food was plentiful, with enough to go around to all the lost souls who wandered in for warmth and nourishment. They weren't more than a minute into their meal when one of the volunteers came around again, trying to give away the leftover rolls. Sid and Alexandra both graciously accepted one extra each.

"Thanks," said Sid. "They're hitting the spot."

"We're hoping to provide even more in the coming months," said the young man distributing the bread. "I hear the fundraiser went well. The kitchen staff already has big plans for next week's menu."

The mention of a fundraiser grabbed Sid's attention.

"Wait, which Mission is this?" he asked.

"The Cartier Bridge Mission," came the reply. "We just opened."

Sid knew of the various soup kitchens in the area, but never bothered to differentiate them. He'd chosen this one because it was the closest.

"Looks like we're dining out on the Mannings again," he chortled.

He had to laugh at happenstance.

"You've been here before?" asked the volunteer.

"First time. But we were at the black-tie gala in Westmount two nights ago."

"Of course you were," the man said. It was a kind but patronizing tone. There was no call to refute the delusions of mentally ill street dwellers.

Sid and Alexandra were both cackling like mad people when he left them to their meal.

"At least the Mannings give you a vegetarian option here," said Sid, as he slurped down his pea-and-carrot soup. He'd nearly drained the bowl before Alexandra reminded him he'd been issued a spoon.

"Right," he said, remembering his manners, and used the spoon to push his spare bun under the surface and drown it. He chopped up the soaked bread with the edge of the utensil and popped one dripping piece into his mouth at a time with his fingers.

"All better?" he asked, once Alexandra had caught up with him and filled her grumbling stomach.

"Better, but not all. I'm still exhausted," she said.

"If we linger for a couple of more hours, we can be first in line for a bed."

"You want me to bunk down in a shelter?" she exclaimed, too loud, too dismayed. Some of the more situationally aware hard-timers looked her way and frowned.

"Or you could check us into The Ritz with that wad of cash you have stuffed in your bra," said Sid.

For a moment, Alexandra thought Sid was accusing her of holding out on him.

"What wad of cash?"

"Exactly."

The point was taken. They were dead broke—not even worth the clothes on their back, which had ceased to have any value whatsoever. Alexandra felt ashamed of herself. She'd lived the high life and the low life since she'd landed in Montreal. Right now she knew she should be grateful for food, a bed, and a roof. She should have been grateful to be alive at all.

"Nobody back home ever finds out I spent the night in a homeless shelter, got it?" Alexandra firmly insisted.

"Who am I going to tell?" asked Sid. "I cut all ties. Besides, I only ever dished dirt on famous people. You're nobody."

"Gee, thanks," said Alexandra, glumly.

"I meant that as a compliment. From one nobody to another."

Alexandra scraped the bottom of her bowl for the last drop of soup.

"You know, Sid, for an ex-paparazzo, you're a hell of detective."

Sid didn't know how to take a compliment either, so he tried not to.

"I'm not exactly hardboiled," he muttered.

"Maybe not, but you're a good egg just the same."

There were two dormitories in The Mission, male and female, set up in two different wings, separated by plenty of doors and corridors so there would be no hanky-panky or worse. That didn't make either Sid or Alexandra safe from some of the more troubled cases who came looking to spend a warm night off the cold streets.

Alexandra was shown the way to the women's dorm as the evening arrived. Inside, she found her bunkmates to be a mix of the disenfranchised, the socio-economic casualties of the city, and the just plain batshit crazy. She expected Sid was fitting in better on his end of the building. He was already a combination of all of the above.

A TV was set up in the corner to keep the ladies amused before they were shut in for the night. Alexandra kept her eyes on it, hoping for a news break that might mention the bombing at Sid's place, or one of the murders she'd been an unwitting party to. Despite a number of channel changes and arguments about which one to watch, she mostly only caught chunks of the same hockey game, in English and French, with various running commentaries that didn't make the violent battle for a puck any more comprehensible. Apparently it was the only local current event that anybody gave a damn about.

Alexandra turned in before the game was over, choosing a bed that was away from the mutterers and the shut-ins, and nearer the chatty girls. She hoped they wouldn't keep her up half the night talking, but at least what they were saying didn't sound insane. One of the older ones tried to bring Alexandra into the conversation.

"What's a pretty thing like you doin' in here?" she asked.

Judging from the woman's outfit of too-tight leather made even tighter by her failing figure, and fishnet stockings that couldn't hope to keep her legs warm or make them look sexy, Alexandra figured her for a budget prostitute long past her prime.

"You still got yer looks," said the woman. "There's plenty-a-men who'll still pay you fer it."

"I'll take that career path under advisement," said Alexandra, pulling back the sheets.

"You think yer too good ta turn a trick?"

"Believe me, these days I feel like a biggest whore in town."

The matron of the mission bellowed, "Lights out ladies!"

The overheads snapped off, leaving Alexandra sitting on her cot in the dark. Everyone else started to settle in for the night, but she remained seated upright and staring at the destitute strangers who surrounded her on all sides. She found one homeless woman in the next cot was staring right back at her.

"Those are pretty shoes," commented the bag lady.

"Touch them and I'll cut you," said Alexandra.

Fireworks

December 31st

IT WAS A crisp new day. The mission opened its doors to send the rest of last night's occupants on their way after a modest but nourishing breakfast. With a chill in the air, everyone got busy buttoning and zipping up their second- and third-hand coats.

Alexandra's bag-lady roomie joined her on the sidewalk and breathed in deeply, sniffing the air, checking the sky.

"Storm's comin'," she announced.

"How can you tell?" asked Alexandra, looking up and seeing nothing but building tops and a few clouds.

"Old bones," said the old woman. "I can feel it in my joints."

She winked and grimaced at Alexandra—her version of a parting smile—and headed off. Alexandra explained the relationship to Sid once he joined her outside.

"We bonded."

"Shared addiction?" asked Sid.

"Shoes," said Alexandra.

Not everyone who'd spent the night in the shelter was so elderly. Alexandra sadly observed one single mother zipping up her little girl and pulling on a tuque that was decorated with a colourful pom-pom on top. The mom was a young woman, slightly hard looking, but maybe only resilient. Alexandra didn't mean to stare, but she was so familiar. It took a while to place her. The last time she saw that face, it had been glazed.

Sid followed Alexandra as she walked over to address the mother.

"Weren't you one of Santa's little helpers?" she asked, recalling the duo of elf thespians who had given St. Nick his signature rosy red cheeks.

"Oh, hey," said the woman. "You two visited the set the other day, right?"

"That was us," admitted Sid.

"I heard you were supposed to be big shots from L.A. What are you doing in this place?"

"Turns out Hollywood isn't the only town that will chew you up and spit you out if you give it half the chance," said Alexandra.

"Sorry," shrugged the woman. "I guess that's show business."

"It sure is," agreed Alexandra. "How about you... Tiffany, was it?"

"Andrea," she said. "Tiffany D. Lite is my stage name."

"My mommy's a movie star," beamed the little girl.

"Congratulations," Alexandra told her.

"I'm going to be a movie star, too."

Alexandra drew back her lips in a thin attempt to smile.

"Make mommy proud," she said.

"You bring your kid to a por..." Sid caught himself. "On an adult shoot with you?"

"Of course not," said Andrea. "Poontang Posse offers daycare. It's in a whole other building. You'd be surprised how many of the MILFs really are mothers."

"Does the job not pay?" asked Alexandra, looking back at the homeless shelter.

"It pays fine," Andrea told her. "It's just not regular work. We take the bus from Guelph. Not a lot of adult shoots in Guelph, so I commute. We crash in a shelter when they call me in. Saves the cost of staying in a motel. More take-home since the bus ticket already eats a chunk of my payday."

"I wouldn't expect another call from Marty anytime soon," said Sid.

Andrea shook her head in disgust, like she had already guessed the news.

"I told him some of that shit he was shooting was crossing the line as far as the obscenity laws are concerned, but he said, 'Oh no! Consenting adults can do whatever they want and watch whatever they want.' Well, not so much if those pricks in Ottawa get their way. So what happened? He get busted?"

"He got killed."

"For reals?" Andrea was surprised but not shocked. "Did he resist arrest or something?"

"It wasn't cops. It was somebody else in the business."

"Competition?"

"Of a sort."

"Jeezus H." said Andrea. "There's so much smut out there, who gives a shit about competition anymore?"

"Can't you get a regular job closer to where you live?" asked Alexandra. "Waitressing maybe."

"Yeah. My day job. Just like a real actor. I take a day or two off to make the round trip when there's a shoot. A thousand bucks a scene. Maybe two scenes on the same trip. Nobody tips that big back home."

"I guess that's over now," said Alexandra apologetically.

"There's always another producer out there. The business is a bottomless pit and it's always hungry for more product. I'll ask around. Someone's bound to be hiring."

"That's the spirit," said Sid. "Get your résumé out there."

"Oh, it's out there. It's out there forever, on every pirate site and file-sharing service. For now and for all time. I'll be old and grey and my great-great-great grandkids will still be able to download videos of me in my youth, selling my ass for a grand a pop to make a better life for them."

Alexandra couldn't tell if Andrea sounded proud or regretful.

With no other destination in mind, Sid and Alexandra joined Andrea and her daughter on their stroll up to Montreal Central Station. She had a couple of return tickets on a Greyhound printed out in her purse, and an hour to spare before the next departure to Guelph, Ontario, by way of a dozen other stops. As they made the trip, Sid took the opportunity to fish for useful information. Although Andrea's knowledge of the inner workings of Marty Guerin's business was thin, she'd overheard plenty of shop talk between takes as Tiffany D. Lite. A half-remembered name and a partial address for the linchpin distribution centre for pornographic books, magazines and videos was buried in her brain, and by the time they arrived at the station, Sid was sure he'd extracted just enough fragments to find it with some more low-tech digging.

With her bus idling in the lot, minutes away from beginning its long milk-run, Andrea made an earnest offer to Alexandra.

"If you want, I could spot you the price of a ticket to another town down the T-Can. One that's not such a chew-you-up spit-you-out sort of place. You could start over, get out of the business. Waitressing isn't so bad. Especially if you've got a partner bringing in a second wage."

Andrea looked at Sid, assuming him to be the significant other who was sticking with Alexandra through thick and thin. Alexandra decided not to refute that fantasy.

"That's very generous," she answered, "but I can't take your money. If you want to keep anybody out of the business, keep her out of it."

Alexandra gave a playful tug on the little girl's pom-pom. Andrea's daughter looked up at her and grinned.

Passengers were boarding the bus as the last of the luggage was loaded and locked in.

"You sure? Last chance."

Alexandra only let herself play with the idea for a moment. It was, she had to admit, an appealing moment.

"I have to see this through. It's what I do," she said.

▶ ▶▌

Sid and Alexandra had to walk ten blocks before they found a public phone booth that had been spared the cell-phone cull. Now that everybody had decided they couldn't live without a smart phone, the public pay phone was nearly extinct. A few had survived to service people with dead batteries or misplaced devices, but they were rare. Rarer still was a phone booth that still had its white and yellow pages hanging from a squat steel counter inside. It took three booths and another dozen blocks before Sid and Alexandra found one.

After hunting for the right section and running down the alphabetical listing of businesses and services that were too cheap, modest or incognito to pay for a bigger box ad, Sid tore out a single sheet of the Yellow Pages and joined Alexandra outside.

"It's in an industrial park off the Trans-Canada," he said, laying a mental map of the island over the address printed on the page.

"Can we get there?"

Sid counted the pocket change he had left in his pocket. It didn't take long. He had one nickel and one dime.

"I couldn't even call them for this much. Bus fare is out of the question unless we pick a street corner and beg for quarters."

"I'm not putting my hat out," insisted Alexandra. "I don't even have a hat to put out."

"We could busk. How's your singing voice? I won't ask you to dance."

"How far is it to walk?"

"Can you make it on those?" he asked of her heeled shoes. She'd already done far more walking than such footwear was designed to endure in a life-time of soirees.

"It'll be rough, but they'll make my blisters look good once we're there."

"It's a long hike. It'll be an even longer one back."

"If we come back," Alexandra said grimly. "I'm worried, Sid."

"We'll be okay," said Sid, putting a hand on her shoulder, comfortingly.

"About the cats," Alexandra clarified. "You think they'll be all right by themselves? They don't even have anything to eat."

"They're cats," Sid reassured her. "They'll make do somehow."

▶▶▌

Far away, in a motel room with a Do-Not-Disturb sign hanging from the door knob, lay two cats curled up together in the middle of the double bed. They slept the day away contently, their thirst quenched, their hunger sated, next to a clear-glass bowl on a bordering end table that was vacant but for a gallon of water and a lingering aftertaste of fish.

▶▶▌

By the end of their journey, the sun had set again, and what had started as an urban hike had turned into a gruelling death march. Sid and Alexandra had to stop multiple times along the way for rest and a foot massage before soldiering on, broke and destitute, towards their final goal.

The route had taken them from the downtown core, to a boulevard that ran straight up the side of a foul-smelling highway trench. Shops and residences gave way to corporate headquarters and finally, above another intersecting highway that cut through the heart of the city, to industry.

The industrial park was a barren, unwelcoming place, even without the winter cold and the tiny squares of dead decorative grass turned brown with the season. Sid and Alexandra were the sole foot traffic, and the only other sign of life was the occasional 18-wheeler rumbling by with new product to sell to the rest of the country. Alexandra let Sid act as pathfinder. The low, boxy buildings all looked alike to her, and the street names were French-Canadian gobbledegook.

When Sid stopped and let her rest her sore feet for the last time, it was pitch-black out but for the streetlights and the orange glow of the city reflecting off the clouds above. The sky was clearing with a stiff wind that was promising a new cold front that would tax their poor choice of winter attire. They were outside a vast warehouse depot with a pothole-laden parking lot that was populated by a scant few employee cars. No trucks were at the loading bays, but all the lights were on, and workers could be seen inside moving pallets of goods around with forklifts.

"This is it," Sid said, double-checking the address on his strip of Yellow Page. "Smut central. Every fuck vid and wank rag produced in Montreal goes through here before being scattered across the globe.

If Helen's sex tape ran through Marty's duplication facilities, this is where the final product went."

There were too many men working the floor for Alexandra's comfort.

"What do we do?" she wondered. "Ask for a guided tour?"

A bell sounded inside the warehouse—a ring long enough to be annoying, and impossible to ignore. The workers all dropped what they were doing and began to disperse to the exits.

"No," said Sid. "We wait for that. It's lunch hour for the night shift. Everyone's heading out to the hotdog joint across the street."

A bright green sign beckoned from the other side of the nearby artery of traffic, promising poutine and steamers that would get around to stopping your heart one day if they didn't choke you first. There was a pedestrian overpass close enough to make it the lunch of least resistance to everyone who clocked hours in the vicinity. Within five minutes, the staff had thinned out considerably, but there were still a few milling about the open cargo-bay doors.

"What about the stragglers?" asked Alexandra, when she saw the brown-baggers weren't leaving.

"It's just like crashing a party," said Sid, reminding Alexandra of her own strategy in such circumstances. "Look like you belong there and everyone will figure you do."

▶▶▮

Once they were sure everybody who was going was gone, Sid and Alexandra strolled right past a trio of workers having a smoke outside on the loading dock. Sid went as far as to nod a greeting and offer them a wave. No one lifted a finger to stop them, nobody asked them what their business was. Sid winked at Alexandra, vindicated, and a moment later they were inside.

The warehouse floor was vast and open, but felt cramped and narrow regardless. It was a full house of merchandise, waiting to be shipped. Hundreds of wooden pallets, towering with shrink-wrapped and strapped-down goods, were lined up in an uneven grid extending to the four corners of the building. Each stack contained bundles of porn magazines, soft core and hard and every degree in between, or the latest DVD releases catering to every kink and quirk. The monoliths of smut loomed high above Sid and Alexandra on all sides, creating narrow corridors and passages that promised a labyrinth should they be foolish enough to step too many rows deep.

Sid stared in awe. "It's like the halls of Valhalla for auto-erotic enthusiasts."

It was impossible to know where to start looking, so Sid and Alexandra split up and wandered through the main passages at random, checking manifests and inventory listings where they could find them.

"Eight thousand, six thousand, twelve thousand..." echoed Alexandra's voice up through the steel rafters overhead.

"What are you counting?" Sid called back to her.

"Units," she said. "The DVDs seem to average around ten thousand copies each. I'm trying to figure out the logistics of getting Helen's flick out of here if we find it."

Stealing that many discs was only one problem. Renting a truck without any cash or credit and then loading it was another that seemed insoluble.

As Sid and Alexandra continued their search, they hardly took note of the sound of the cargo-bay doors rattling down their tracks and closing, sealing them in. Alexandra nearly commented on the final bang as corrugated steel met concrete, but then Sid interrupted her with the announcement, "I think this is it!"

Alexandra zigzagged her way out of the maze and joined Sid at the pallet he'd discovered. The massive bundles of DVDs were held together by enormous sheets of plastic wrap and tight nylon straps. Sid sawed through the wrapping with his house keys, making a tear big enough to pull a single DVD free from the stack underneath. The crudely Photoshopped cover for the quickie release showed various shots, suggestively cropped, of Helen, screen-captured from the original video, under the garish and topical title, "Take It From Behind: The Helen St. Simone Sex Tape."

Having confirmed they had the goods, Alexandra took a step back to mentally measure the size of the task at hand.

"Yeah, that's it," she agreed. "And there's a lot of it, isn't there? Okay, okay. Thinking..."

Sid read the manifest that was fixed with packing tape to one corner of the first block of merchandise.

"Think fast," he said. "It ships tomorrow morning."

Alexandra was working out how a miracle could be accomplished given her current impoverished state. But she came from a town that made magic happen all the time, often on a tight budget, sometimes with no budget at all. Mountains could be moved with a bit of ingenuity and, better yet, friends with an expense account.

"If I can make a collect call out of here, I can get one of the staff back home to wire me funds. We'll eat all the fees we have to to make it happen first thing in the morning. Then we'll need to pay some people to look the other way, and more to help us load the goods. We can get a U-Haul rental or maybe even a chartered bus or..."

"Better make it a whole convoy," said Sid, just as Alexandra was about to convince herself it was feasible. "Check this out."

Sid tore the manifest off the block of cargo and held it out for Alexandra, his finger pointing to the top of the page. She squinted at the number buried among all the weights and measurements and destinations. It was many digits long.

"Is that a phone number?" she asked.

"It's a unit total," said Sid.

Alexandra looked at Sid and felt the colour draining from her face. She had wondered how they had found a single sad piece of smut in the midst of this forest of pornography so easily, so quickly. Without saying a word, she walked around the corner of the packed pallet and headed down the long corridor of merchandise beyond. She started at a brisk pace and ended in a full-out run before reaching the end. The entire length of one wall of the warehouse—totalling at least a third of the entire floor space—was devoted to copies of Helen's sex tape. There were hundreds of thousands of units at least. Maybe more than a million. Marty Guerin's mill must have been churning out copies all week long.

Alexandra slowly sank to the floor, sitting down heavily on one free corner of a wooden pallet reserved for another, less promising erotica title. Holding her head in her hands, she didn't know whether to laugh or cry. Sid eventually caught up with her and tried to say something reassuring, or at least comforting.

"It never rains, it pours, right?"

On that note, Sid felt a random drop of liquid land on his cheek. He wiped it off and rubbed the drop between his fingers.

"Hey," he said, "it *is* raining."

Alexandra held her hand out, feeling for precipitation indoors. A few more drops landed in her own palm. She sniffed at the liquid and quickly became alarmed.

"This isn't water. It's gasoline!"

They both looked up at the same time and saw Franklin, high above them, making his way down the catwalk that ran close to the roof, pouring the contents of a large gas can over the side of the railing and onto the row of pallets below.

As Sid and Alexandra gaped at the act of arson in progress, they failed to notice Louise Manning arrive behind them.

"My dear Miss Middleton," she said, startling her and Sid both, "you've spent so much time and effort trying to put out this Helen St. Simone sex-tape fire, it seems the only way to be rid of the damn thing is for me to start an even bigger one."

"Louise?" said Sid, once he saw the Manning matriarch before him. "Really?"

"Who else were you expecting?" asked Louise.

"I figured it must be your husband running the numbers behind your piece of the porno pie."

Louise found Sid's notion amusing.

"We'd be living on the street if I let my fool of a husband handle our finances," she scoffed. "He'd have it invested in banks and car companies and capital lenders. But I always knew there was only one industry that could weather any recession. The sex industry. People will live without a roof over the heads or food in their stomachs before they give up a glimpse of tits and ass."

"Funny," commented Sid. "I know an enterprising young stripper who was telling us the same thing, just the other day."

"Women in this line of work always seem to have a better head for business," said Louise. "It was the same back when I was in pasties. Let the old-boys club of financial advisors and economist gamblers bet on the markets. I only bet on a sure thing, like the simple basic human sex drive."

Franklin finished dousing the pallets with gasoline and tossed the empty can away.

"You're burning it all?" asked Alexandra. "I thought your thugs wanted to get their hands on it the whole time."

"Good Lord, why?" asked Louise, incredulously.

"Because it's worth a fortune," suggested Alexandra.

"Nonsense. It will bankrupt us all in the end."

Sid and Alexandra looked confused, so Louise explained.

"The more mainstream pornography becomes, the worse off we'll all be. These idiot celebrities know no shame. They're ruining pornography for the honest sex worker. If all these ridiculous fame-whores keep letting their private sex tapes get out, where will that leave the rest of us? Who will want to pay to see anonymous bodies and nameless faces perform explicit acts when they can watch last year's Best Actress Oscar recipient blow a two-time Emmy winner while a triple-platinum Grammy runner-up fucks her in the ass? This sort of thing is killing the business and all evidence of it must be stamped out, obliterated, erased before it sees the light of day."

Sid was unconvinced.

"You really think suppressing one celebrity sex tape is going to eliminate your competition from superstar scabs?"

"No," admitted Louise, "but it will keep the dam from bursting for just a little while longer."

Alexandra wasn't having any of it. Louise Manning's financial model had wrought too much violence, too many deaths.

"Was murder always a part of the sex trade? You know, a thousand years ago, back when you were in pasties?"

Louise considered that for a moment before noting, "Sex and violence have always gone hand-in-hand. There's more money in both that way."

"Franklin," she called to her man on the catwalk, "finish off the witnesses before you torch the place. I'll be waiting in the car."

Louise Manning turned to leave as Franklin slid down an access ladder and landed between Sid and Alexandra.

"Plan?" Alexandra asked Sid desperately.

"Run!" was Sid's only suggestion.

Alexandra agreed with that course of action. Together, she and Sid dashed into the web of merchandise, determined to lose themselves, even as Franklin chased after them in hot pursuit.

Arriving at the opposite wall of the warehouse, Louise pressed the button to close the final remaining cargo-bay door. She ducked under as it slid down into place. Once outside, she lit a cigarette and waited to hear the door lock behind her. There was a drainage pipe leading from the warehouse right next to the exit. A swirling rainbow of fuel-tinted water had already formed in the puddle under the mouth of the pipe, and a distinct gasoline odour rose from the gate underfoot.

"Oh, what the hell," she said to herself, making the latest in a string of ruthless business decisions. "I can always drive myself."

Louise tossed the lit match into the grate in the pavement and left. The gasoline collecting inside ignited with a pop, and flames followed the trail back into the heart of the warehouse. Moments later, fires began to spring up from various drains set in the foundation that were meant to keep the floor dry when the weather blew in or boots tracked rain and snow inside. Now, each of them had become their own barbeque pit, licking at the closest pallets, trying to pass the flames on to the next available fuel.

When the grate nearest the back wall lit up, the fire had an easy time finding the nearest splashes of spilled gasoline. It hopscotched its way from spill to puddle until it lit up the entire stock of Helen St. Simone sex tapes, coughing toxic black smoke into the air as the plastic wrap burned away quickly and let the flames take hold of the denser kindling underneath.

As a column of flames erupted behind them, Alexandra pulled ahead of the foot race. Franklin, however, closed in on Sid's tail, remaining focused on his target even as the nearby stacks of DVDs violently ignited one after the other.

Sid turned sharply and darted down another corridor of merchandise. He took his keys out again and tore into the plastic wrapping to one side, hardly slowing as he cut a slit through several pallets worth of goods.

Franklin got within arm's reach of Sid as they rounded the next corner, but no closer. As Sid dove to the floor, Franklin failed to duck in time to avoid running face-first into the base of a fire extinguisher. The blow sent him reeling backwards onto the floor. He only got a glimpse of Alexandra wielding the extinguisher before she turned it on him and sprayed a few short bursts into his face, blinding him.

Sid scrambled to his feet, ran a few paces down the parallel alley, and rammed his shoulder into the tower of porn DVDs. It took a few blows to dislodge the tightly packed discs, but once the cascade began, the merchandise came spilling out of the slit he'd made in the plastic wrap on the opposite side. Thousands of DVDs ruptured out of the breach like a bursting pimple. Franklin, still scraping the fire repellant foam out of his eyes, tried to raise his hands defensively, but was quickly buried under a ton of shrink-wrapped slip cases. Sid and Alexandra left him behind, pinned and lost under an avalanche of porn, as they hurried to the nearest cargo-bay door.

The flames were spreading to other rows and Alexandra had to squeeze off the occasional shot from the extinguisher she'd acquired to clear the path for them. Once the fire found a foothold in the first throng of skin rags and X-rated magazines, the blaze upgraded itself to an inferno.

At the sealed door, Sid and Alexandra found their escape thwarted by a key pad. The buttons were there to operate the door, but they proved more complex than a simple toggle switch. A few random stabs at the numbers proved futile.

"We need a code!" Alexandra concluded.

"No," said Sid. "We need a ram."

He ran off, back towards the encroaching flames. Alexandra briefly lost sight of Sid in the billowing smoke, but spotted him again a moment later as he leapt into the driver's seat of a forklift and started it up. Alexandra ran to join him, hopping on the back as he swung the vehicle around and gunned it, aiming at the bay door.

Sid lowered the forks to floor level as he tried to reach ramming speed. The forklift didn't have much pickup in it, and its top speed proved too slow. Sid tried to spur it faster as it raced down the burning corridor, but when it finally made impact on the thick metal sheeting of the door, it didn't have enough momentum to do more than cause the whole structure to wobble violently in its tracks. Sid and Alexandra were thrown from the vehicle and landed, bruisingly, on the concrete floor.

Sid, lying flat on his belly, saw that the two forks of the lift had at least managed to tear through the bottom edge of the door. He hurried back to the controls of the forklift and tried to jack it up manually. His inspired attempt only managed to peel away twin strips of ridged metal, tearing two large gashes in the door that were far too narrow to squeeze through.

Sid and Alexandra went to the holes they'd made and stuck their faces through, sucking in a few lungfuls of fresh outdoor air. The smoke inside was quickly getting too thick to breathe. As they spared a gasping moment together, they heard the first sirens of approaching fire engines.

"Here comes the cavalry," Sid noted.

"If they hurry, they might still be able to identify our remains by the dental records," said Alexandra.

"Joke's on them," chuckled Sid humourlessly. "I haven't been to a dentist in thirty years."

The flames were spreading fast, climbing the walls and probing through the roof. All the burning plastic, laminated pages, and digital media were letting off noxious fumes that were threatening to choke the life out of Sid and Alexandra. Desperate for any other exit, Sid scanned the warehouse as far as the smoke would allow, and pointed to a spot on the floor a couple of dozen yards away.

"There!" he shouted. "We need to clear a path."

Alexandra retrieved her abandoned fire extinguisher and sprayed at a few problem spots as they made their way to a large iron trap door set into the concrete. Larger than any of the drainage grates meant to deal with leaks and spills, this one allowed access to the building's plumbing system. Sid strained to raise the metal cover and finally managed to tip it over with a deafening clatter, exposing the main line.

"What is it?" Alexandra asked.

"A way out!" said Sid, adding, "Possibly. I think."

Alexandra looked down into the pipe yawning open below her. It was a horrid, slimy mess.

"Are you kidding me? That's a sewer pipe!"

Sid was reasonably sure it wasn't a direct connection to the city sewer system, but it was filthy enough to suggest it might be. He gave himself a 50/50 chance of coming out the other side somewhere near a ladder or manhole that would get him back to the surface before he found himself washed away to a sewage-treatment plant on the other side of the island.

"I think I can squeeze through," he speculated. "I'll follow it out and open the door from the other side. Wait here!"

Before Alexandra could argue with him, Sid dove head-first into the pipe and wriggled away into the ooze.

▶▶▌

The first of the fire trucks had arrived and the crew was attaching their hose to the nearest hydrant. By the time more turned onto the street, answering the four-alarm call to additional stations, the firefighters already on the scene were dousing the warehouse with a steady stream of water, soaking the site to keep the flames from leaping to other nearby buildings. The noise of multiple sirens filled the air, louder than any New Year's Eve celebrations elsewhere in the city.

Louise tried to appear nonchalant as she let herself into her car. It was the only non-emergency vehicle remaining on the property. The night-shift skeleton crew had all since hurried back to move their own cars a safe distance away from what was fast becoming a disaster area.

Not more than a few feet underfoot, Sid was squeezing his way through the pipe, soaking himself in putrid sludge with each inch gained. On his last push, he managed to wedge himself inside with his arms pinned to his sides. He struggled to squirm free, but found he couldn't advance or retreat from the position he was stuck in.

"Nrrrrrrgg!" Sid roared. "Goddammit!"

Sid looked ahead, down the inky black passage. There was just enough light filtering through from behind for him to see a large rat in his path. It had come from the other end of the pipe and, finding Sid blocking his way, sat up on its hind legs to observe him.

"Run, Lassie!" Sid instructed it. "Go get help!"

Alexandra blasted a circle around herself with the extinguisher, trying to hold onto her diminishing piece of flame-free real estate. It was a losing battle.

Aluminum sheeting from the roof began to cave into the warehouse below, weakened by the cascading torrent above and the blasting heat below. Water from the fire hoses rained down and Alexandra moved to get under the shower, but it was doing little to stem to spread of the fire. As she backed away from the intense furnace, she was unaware that she had arrived back at the spot where Franklin lay buried under DVD cases. By then, the inferno was roaring so loudly, she couldn't hear the pile behind her shift as Franklin freed himself from the weight that pinned him.

Sid remained hopelessly stuck in his position. Struggling as much as he could, the pipe had him thoroughly lodged. His one-rat audience watched indifferently.

"Wipe that smart-ass look off your face or I'll introduce you my cat," Sid told the vermin.

"Actually, I think you could take him," Sid said, noting the exceptional size of the rat. "My cat's a pussy."

Franklin rose from the mound of debris and snuck up behind Alexandra. He was almost on her when she spun around and aimed the fire extinguisher at him.

"Back off!" she commanded.

Franklin was amused by the threat. Alexandra's last shot from the extinguisher had been no more than a momentary distraction.

"Or what?" he sneered.

"Or I won't put you out."

Franklin stopped to consider Alexandra's words. A moment later, he realized the back of his coat was on fire. He panicked and began running in circles, trying to get away from the blaze.

"Get down! Get down!" Alexandra shouted at him.

Franklin dropped to the floor and rolled around, trying to smother the flames. Alexandra expended the last of the extinguisher's contents putting out his burning clothes. Saved from anything worse than superficial scorching, Franklin rose, soaked in fire retardant, and double checked that he'd been put out.

"Thanks!" he declared, genuinely grateful, and then proceeded to wrap his fingers around Alexandra's throat.

►►|

Louise had the car started, but she was fumbling with the stick shift, trying to get it in gear. It had been decades since she last drove herself anywhere. It was coming back to her, just not quickly. She decided to blame advancing technology over advancing age.

Meanwhile, more fire engines were arriving, threatening to block her path. There were already three engines hooked up to two different fire hydrants, blasting the warehouse with thousands of gallons of water. Multiple waterfalls were pouring into the warehouse through the wrecked roof. Despite the huge volume of water thrown at the problem, it was failing to do more than keep the conflagration from spreading to the rest of the block.

Franklin and Alexandra fought each other inside, even as the whole place was starting to collapse around them. A knee to the groin finally got Franklin to release his grip and Alexandra was able to push him off her.

"Keep away from me!" she warned, grabbing the spent fire extinguisher again and raising it over her head.

"Give me your best shot," Franklin challenged her.

Alexandra hurtled the canister at him, but it was easily sidestepped. She watched her last line of defence clatter away into the smoke and destruction. Franklin smiled, and that flash of teeth was the last Alexandra saw of him. A moment later, the first falling steel girder obliterated his skull. He vanished under a huge section of roof that collapsed after sagging to the breaking point under the weight of all the water collecting on it.

A huge flood came down with the roof, sweeping Alexandra off her feet and overwhelming the warehouse's drainage system in an instant.

Sid's rodent acquaintance suddenly turned around in the pipe and fled at a full scamper.

"Lassie?" Sid called after it. "What's wrong, girl?"

A tremendous rush of water hit Sid from behind a moment later, dislodging him and blasting him forward. Fifty yards and only moments later, he popped out the far end like a cork and landed in a drainage ditch at the side of the road. Sid came sputtering and gasping out of the pool of muck and dirty water and crawled up the low embankment. He found himself at the edge of the warehouse property and saw the building was now a wall of intense orange and red, barely distinguishable behind all the flames. It didn't look like it would last much longer.

"Alex," he said aloud, and began running.

Sid wove through the phalanx of yellow helmets and coats, trying to get someone's attention as the firefighters coordinated the effort to contain the fire.

"Guys! Guys! There's someone still in there!" he pleaded.

A chief from one of the summoned stations was the only one who could spare a moment to address Sid.

"The whole structure is unsound," he was told. "I can't risk sending any of my men inside until it's under control."

Sid was left wandering among the engines and hoses, looking for anyone else in the entire industrial park who could help.

▶▶❘

Louise had just managed to get her car into gear when the driver's door popped open.

"Franklin?" she asked.

"Scoot over, honey," said Sid. "We're going for a ride."

Sid shoved Louise Manning over into the passenger seat, got behind the wheel, and buckled up. Louise failed to follow his example and went flying as Sid peeled away. Whipping around various emergency vehicles on the lot sent the brittle old woman bouncing all over the interior of the car until Sid straightened out and aimed at one of the cargo-bay doors. He floored it, propelling Louise back into her seat face-first.

Inside, Alexandra was hacking from all the smoke. Keeping low to the floor was doing nothing at this point. The fumes were everywhere, as were the flames that had her surrounded on all sides.

Suddenly, one of the bay doors imploded on impact as Louise's car burst into the doomed building. It tore down the length of the wide centre alley and made a sharp quarter turn as it squealed to a halt just short of where Alexandra stood.

The driver's window rolled down and Sid asked, "Going my way, Miss?"

Alexandra considered what she could say that would be cool and aloof—anything not to let on that Sid was her hero at that particular moment in time. She failed.

"Fuck yeah!" was what she came up with.

Alexandra yanked open the rear door and dove in. Sid turned the car around as bits of flaming rubble bounced off the hood, and the rest of the vehicle was heavily peppered with burning embers.

"Please fasten your safety belts and extinguish all smoking materials," Sid announced hurriedly as he listened to the walls buckle.

Alexandra snapped one of the belts in the back around her waist. Louise, a dazed mess, was too stunned to follow the suggestion.

"Wuzzat?" was all she managed to say before she went flying again.

Sid pushed the car to its acceleration limits as flames licked at its sides. More sections of the warehouse collapsed into a heap in its wake. Sid had to turn the wipers on to keep the burning debris off of the windshield. Through the thick haze of smoke, he spotted the hole he'd just made in the door and adjusted his trajectory. An instant later, the car rocketed out of the warehouse and into the open night air.

A safe distance from the inferno, the car slowed to a halt on sizzling, melted tires. Sid and Alexandra let themselves out of the front and rear doors.

Relieved, Alexandra gushed, "Oh, Sid!"

She hugged him in a warm embrace that was touching right up until she got a good whiff of him.

"Oh, Sid!" she repeated, recoiling in disgust.

Auld Lang Syne

January 1st

AMBULANCES AND POLICE were starting to arrive on the scene. Among them was an unmarked car with a flasher blinking red on the dashboard. Inspector Langelier got out on the passenger side and was greeted by an on-site officer who had called him directly. The uniformed man pointed out the luxury car with the tinted windows that was parked on the perimeter of the ongoing calamity. A charred wreck, scraped and dented with an accordioned front grill, it was probably not long out of a junkyard—once it had served its purpose as evidence in police lockup.

"Merci, officier," Langelier told the uniform.

Langelier's partner got out from behind the wheel and joined him.

"Am I a fool," Langelier asked him, "or does that car match the description of the one witnesses placed at the hit-and-run bombing the other day?"

It was a rhetorical question. There had been an APB circulating for the last 48 hours with a detailed description of the car, but no licence plate. Langelier had come prepared to positively identify the vehicle by other means.

After recovering her senses and giving the passenger door a few tries, Louise managed to get it open and stumble out. She couldn't have looked more dishevelled if she'd just stepped off a roller coaster in her soiled Sunday best.

Langelier and his partner were busy inspecting the dent in the rear bumper. The partner was scraping flecks of dried blood out of the chrome and into a plastic evidence bag.

"Madame Manning?" Langelier asked, surprised to see the old woman emerge from the wreck.

Louise took a few unsteady steps away from the car. When she turned around, she was horrified by the state of her luxury drive.

"My car!" she exclaimed.

"*Your* car?" asked Langelier.

Sid sat on the rear stoop of an ambulance and took a final hit from an oxygen tank. His residual cough had subsided, but he was worried about Alexandra. He'd only nearly drowned. She had twice as much time as him to suffer smoke inhalation.

Alexandra came over, a blanket across her shoulders, an oxygen tank in her hand, and a mask on her face. She sat down next to Sid and together they watched the warehouse burn itself out.

"You should go," said Sid, reassured she was all right. The rest of the night in a hospital bed for observation and they'd give her a clean bill of health by noon at the latest. "Check out, move on, never come back. I can handle any questions the cops might have. Your name doesn't even have to come up."

Alexandra peeled the mask off her face and cleared her throat. "I wouldn't leave you holding the bag. I figure somebody's going to want me to come back and testify about something at someone's trial."

Sid figured she was probably right.

"If you need a place to stay when you're back in town," he began, but caught himself.

"Well," he added, "let me know if you find something good. I need a place to stay, too."

"You bet."

Sid and Alexandra sat in silence together, staring at the column of smoke and flame that rose high into the sky. Sparks flew and whipped around in the wind. It was a spectacular show.

"Didn't I promise you fireworks for New Year's?" said Sid.

"No, actually. You didn't," Alexandra recalled.

Sid thought about it and concluded, "No, you're right. I didn't. But wouldn't that have been romantic?"

"Ironic," said Alexandra. "It would have been ironic."

"Ironic, romantic. It's all the same these days."

Langelier and his partner marched Louise over to where Sid and Alexandra sat. She was in handcuffs.

"Good evening, Inspector," said Alexandra.

"Come to roast some chestnuts on an open fire?" said Sid.

"I'm sure you and Monsieur Volke can explain what you're doing here," said Langelier.

"Of course," Alexandra assured him.

"And this isn't your doing?" suggested Langelier.

"Absolutely not," answered Sid.

"You know who started it?"

"He's inside," Alexandra told the Inspector.

Langelier looked at the warehouse and sighed as the walls collapsed, reducing the flaming ruin to a smouldering garbage heap. It would be a hell of a mess to sift through.

"Is that where your videotape is as well?" he asked the couple.

Alexandra didn't answer. Instead, she looked to Louise and raised her eyebrows at the woman. Louise spoke in complete accordance with Alexandra.

"Tape?" stated Louise Manning, "What tape?"

"There's no tape," confirmed Alexandra.

"Never was," agreed Louise.

Snow Job

January 2nd

ALEXANDRA SPENT THE morning shopping. New Year's Day had been a wash, with nearly everything closed, but stores were open again for the second day of the year, and most of them were still having post-Christmas sales. Having put a rush on her replacement cards, they'd arrived at the motel by courier before she was even awake. A few confirmation calls to activate them and she was ready to run up enough debt to finish maxing out the rest of her credit line.

The priority was some travel clothes, remedied by a quick excursion to a nearby West Island mall. There wasn't much to meet her exacting standards right off the rack, but Alexandra was only a five-hour flight away from the rest of her wardrobe, and the Rodeo Drive shops that would be able to replace what she'd lost over the course of her working vacation. Eventually she held her nose and bought a single outfit that wouldn't be too awful to be seen in for a day. She couldn't abide anything on offer in the shoe department and resolved that her lone remaining pair, scuffed and sullied though they'd become, would suffice. Better, she decided, to be seen in shoes that were once a thing of beauty than shoes that were ugly straight out of the box.

Back at the motel, she packed up her luggage—which amounted to little more than Sabrina in her cage—and checked out. It was a short taxi hop up the ramp to the departure gate of Trudeau International. Alexandra buttoned her new winter coat, which she would never need again and expected to donate to a homeless shelter as soon as she got back, and gathered her purse and cat. As she kicked the cab door shut and stepped onto the curb, she saw a single snowflake land on her sleeve. It was a perfect, crystalized flake, intricate in design, delicate in structure. She had never seen one in person before and was surprised, when closely observed, how it looked just like the idealized images of single snowflakes in magazine ads during the winter fashion season. Or like a pattern a child might cut out of a folded piece of white paper for a school arts-and-crafts project.

It was lovely, and Alexandra turned her head up to the sky, hoping to see more. It was cloudy and overcast, but there were no other signs of snow.

Alexandra stood looking out the departure lounge's window at the tarmac, but she couldn't see any tarmac.

Or anything else for that matter. It was a white-out of blowing snow.

She glanced over her shoulder at the flight board in time to see everything flip from departure and arrival times to nothing but cancelled cancelled cancelled.

▶ ▶❚

Alexandra came slogging through the front doors of the motel once more, the same motel she had wished to never see again. She stomped the snow off her soaking-wet feet once she was inside. No designer footwear, she had learned in a very short period of time, was up for a Canadian winter. Approaching the front desk, she faced the manager, busy with a blizzard-and-cancellation influx of clients, and caught his eye.

"So this is snow," said Alexandra, unimpressed.

"Yeah," the manager confirmed.

"It sucks," Alexandra opined.

"Yeah," the manager agreed.

The lobby was packed with stranded passengers, sitting on their bags, trying to phone cabs or family, and watching the weather report on TV.

"Tell me you have a room," Alexandra pleaded.

The managed spared her a familiar smile.

"For you, always."

Alexandra slapped down her pristine gold card with a look of relief. Her other cards were precariously full after a hurried day of new clothes and air fare, but her prized golden boy was still ready to see her through this day.

"Well then, let's pop the cherry on my new plastic."

"Want me to unlock the Adult Entertainment channel in your room?" the manager kindly offered. "No extra charge."

"Hell no," said Alexandra.

"Well if there's anything else I can..."

Alexandra's attention had wandered to the security monitor footage of the parking lot. There was nothing to see. All it showed was blizzard white. For the first time she noticed what was on the shelf right next to the monitor.

"What are those?" she asked.

There was a stack of videotapes behind the desk. They were all loose. None of them had a slip case.

"Nothing too entertaining there," said the manager. "Just the tapes I use for the security-camera feed. You know, whatever's lying around."

Alexandra focused on one tape in the middle of the pack. It had a strip of masking tape down the spine. Handwritten on the label in black felt-tip pen was one word: Dumbo.

Having Kittens

April 4th

IT WAS SUN and sand as usual in Malibu. All the Christmas kitsch had long since been swept away in the weeks following the holidays—replaced by the non-denominational kitsch that usually polluted the vista of wealthy Los Angeles.

Inside the Helen St. Simone compound, away from prying entertainment reporters, celebrity-hunting photographers, and tourist tour buses salivating over the homesteads of the rich and famous, Helen was trying on her wedding dress. A brand-new personal assistant by the name of Maxine was helping her squeeze into it. The new girl was having a hard time fastening the elaborate hooks and latches up the back.

"Goddamn it," Helen hollered as she felt her ribs straining to the breaking point, "I told you I still wasn't at my wedding weight when you ordered this fucking thing!"

Maxine had been on the job a week, but she already knew to speak only when spoken to, and to shut her mouth when she was being yelled at. With less than a month to go, it seemed unlikely Helen was ever going to hit her overly ambitious target weight without liposuction, dehydration and the world's most thorough colonic.

"When the fuck is Cindy getting back?" Helen asked no one specific. "I can't do anything with this imbecile!"

The rest of the regular staff was on hand. Monica, Patrick and Jeffrey were all hard at work with the latest mountain of Helen's personal and professional errands that had bloomed in the New Year and were increasing exponentially as W-Day approached.

"Cindy's not coming back," Patrick reminded her, as he had done every day since January. "She quit."

"Why the fuck would she do that? I was paying her twice as much as I pay this dumbass whatshername."

"Maxine," said Maxine, compelled to fill in the blank.

"Do I look like I give a shit what your fucking name is?"

The fitting was happening in Helen's bedroom, which was so large and stately, Alexandra's arrival passed with hardly any notice. She tipped open the door with a toe of her newest pair of replacement designer shoes and entered, her arms filled with a big box peppered with air holes.

Confirming all the usual suspects in Helen's staff were accounted for, Alexandra announced, "It's nearly Mother's Day. So who wants to be a mother?"

Jeffrey was the first to respond, coming over to remove the top from the box. Inside was a collection of freshly-weaned kittens—an even mix of fluffy white Sabrina and dark shorter-haired Hoagy.

"Oh my God, they're adorable," gushed Jeffrey. "Where did you get them?"

"Um..." Alexandra hesitated, "They're sort of a surprise discovery of mine."

Across the room, Maxine got the last snap fastened. Helen stepped back in her full bridal gown regalia and twirled.

"So what do you think?" she asked.

Maxine waited an instant too long to respond.

Helen cut her off before she could make a sound, "Fuck it! Who gives a shit what you think?"

Her mood softened in a flash the moment she spotted Alexandra and the contents of her box.

"Ooo! Kittens!" Helen cooed.

In her rush to see the new arrivals, she knocked over her bag on the floor. Accessory Dog made a break from his upended prison and fled the room. Helen plucked one of the kittens from the box and cuddled it.

"Can I have one?" she pleaded. "Oh please! Oh pretty please!"

"Okay, one," conceded Alexandra. "Just one."

Helen reconsidered the kitten in her arms and put it back, selecting another bundle of fur she found more aesthetically pleasing. She left the room hugging and kissing it mercilessly.

"You two play nice!" Alexandra called after her.

"You should get that thing declawed first," commented Monica, hardly looking up from her work notes for the day.

"That's a cruel thing to do to a cat," Alexandra scolded.

"I was talking about Helen."

With the boss now out of earshot, Maxine spoke up hesitantly.

"Look," she said, "I know I'm the new kid at school and all. And maybe I'm a bit out of line here, but..."

Maxine considered her words carefully before continuing, "Is she always such a colossal cunt?"

Jeffrey scanned the room until he caught Patrick's eye. They exchanged a look and an instant understanding.

"Dumbo?" suggested Jeffrey.

"Definitely Dumbo," agreed Patrick.

"Guys...no, please," Monica began, but knew her argument against it was already lost.

The new girl had no idea what they were talking about.

"What do you mean, Dumbo?" asked Maxine.

"Dumbo virgin!" declared Patrick, pointing an accusing finger.

"That decides it," stated Jeffrey.

Monica tried to protest, but Patrick swung his finger at her and she fell silent.

"No arguments!" he insisted. "She must be initiated into the fold!"

The staff reconvened in the pool house. Jeffrey dug in the cabinet to find the recently recovered videotape. Patrick retrieved the VCR from the closet and hooked it up. Monica and Alexandra merely submitted to the inevitable.

The key players assembled, Maxine now counted among them, integrated into the extended members of the St. Simone payroll-entourage. Yet again, the sex tape was cued up, and everyone was reunited for the first screening since its flirtation with exposure to the general public.

Jeffrey hit "Play" and the audience was immediately serenaded by the familiar grunts and groans of Helen and her ex. But there was no laughter or mocking this time, only perplexed confusion as they all stared at the television screen.

"What the hell is this?" Patrick demanded.

"I don't know," said Jeffrey, "but it kinda works for me."

The audio remained unchanged, but the image had been taped over with black and white security-camera footage of an airport motel parking lot. Aside from the occasional passing car or pedestrian, the shot remained static, overlaid with increasingly frantic sex noises.

"I like this redux cut better," decided Monica. "The acting's much more convincing."

Alexandra's phone rang. She got up to answer it, removing herself from the screening so she could talk in private.

"How are our children?" asked Sid on the line.

"Surprisingly cute, all things considered," Alexandra said.

Sid wandered through his home, talking on a wireless extension. The place was in mid-renovation following the bomb blast. Holes were being filled, scorch marks painted over. Sid was doing much of the work himself, dressed in paint- and plaster-spattered overalls.

"Has the groom grown a brain and gotten cold feet yet?" he asked.

"I think he's in denial," said Alexandra, "taking it one day at a time. The plan is to get him so drunk at his bachelor party, he won't sober up until the honeymoon."

"Where's this bachelor party happening? I need an address."

"You're not invited."

Sid entered the bedroom. It had managed to escape the brunt of the blast, and gave him a place to crash while he worked to make the apartment livable again. His laundry hamper was still there and he opened the top so he could pick through the clothes inside.

"I've had enough gratuitous nudity to last me a while, believe me," said Sid.

Under the first few layers of clothes, Sid found an old framed photo of Alexandra from a decade earlier—back when she was Alexis. It wasn't a posed shot, nor a candid one, but simply a relaxed, natural moment, walking on the beach in California. He paused to look at it for a moment before he kept digging.

"It's just that I haven't gotten the happy couple a wedding present," he continued. "I don't know where the bride is registered, but I have a little something I think the groom might enjoy."

Deep down, near the very bottom of the hamper, he found what he was looking for. It was a DVD slip case, filthy from the fire and the sewer pipe. The laminated insert was stained but intact, identifying it as the final remaining copy of the Helen St. Simone sex tape.

Release

May 1st

FOR IMMEDIATE RELEASE

SAINT HELEN INCORPORATED
CONTACT: ALEXANDRA MIDDLETON
DATE: MAY 1

Eight months after proposing marriage to stage-and-screen superstar, Helen St. Simone, actor Nick Hadford has called off the wedding, citing irreconcilable differences.

"Helen is a wonderful woman, and I wish her nothing but the best," he said in a statement released on April 30. "After much introspection and heartache, we have agreed not to move forward with our relationship of the last three years."

Helen St. Simone, Oscar Award-winning actress, Grammy Award-winning singer and, most recently, subject of the best-selling biography *Take It from the Top: The Helen St. Simone Story* says the decision was mutual and came from a place of love and profound respect.

"This has been a difficult time for us both," said St. Simone yesterday. "I know my fans will be disappointed by this news. We were all looking forward to a beautiful spring wedding, but it simply wasn't meant to be. Life is full of unexpected twists and turns, and sometimes incompatibility issues outweigh love. Moving forward, Nick and I hope to remain close friends and a mutual source of emotional support and guidance as we forge ahead with our separate lives and careers."

This would have been the fourth marriage for St. Simone and the third for Hadford.

CONTACT DETAILS FOLLOW (PAGE 2)

Acknowledgements

The author wishes to thank Kathryn Presner, Ellie Presner, Michael Brodie, and Kirsten LM for all due diligence in the bug hunt; David Lascelle for the lengthy discussions about high concepts and low life; the underground writers and directors of the porno-chic era who tried to elevate adult cinema; and all the mainstream celebrities of the home-video era who dragged it right back down again with their candid carnality.

About the Author

Shane Simmons is an award-winning screenwriter and graphic novelist whose work has appeared in international film festivals, museums and lectures about design and structure. His art has been discussed in multiple books and academic journals about sequential storytelling, and his short stories have been printed in critically praised anthologies of history, crime and horror. He lives in Montreal with his wife and too many cats.

Also by Shane Simmons

<u>Novels</u>

Necropolis
Filmography

<u>Collections</u>

Raw and Other Stories

<u>Booklets</u>

Carrion Luggage
Hot Pennies
Choke the Chicken
The Red Baron: An Ace for the Ages

<u>Graphic Novels</u>

The Long and Unlearned Life of Roland Gethers
The Failed Promise of Bradley Gethers
The Inauspicious Adventures of Filson Gethers

Last Words

Small-press publishers rely on reviews from readers like you to help get the word out about their books. Whether it's a simple star rating or a written critique, every bit of feedback helps convince the impersonal computer algorithms of Amazon, and other literary outlets, that the book you just read has merit and deserves more exposure. Please support independent authors, editors and publishers by taking a few moments to share your thoughts and opinions with other potential readers who may be sitting on the fence about trying an intriguing novel or collection. Your suggestions or comments can make all the difference when it comes to helping them find a new writer they'll like, or matching a struggling author with the readership he or she deserves. Thank you.

www.ingramcontent.com/pod-product-compliance
Lightning Source LLC
Chambersburg PA
CBHW030325200626
46816CB00006BA/1927